M. Ruth Myers is a practising magician living in Ohio. *A Touch of* … thrillers with a m… Stuart.

A Touch of Magic

M. Ruth Myers

HEADLINE

First published in Great Britain in 1989
by HEADLINE BOOK PUBLISHING PLC

Portions of this book were first published in
Good Housekeeping (US edition) August 1987

ISBN 0 7472 3206 7

Printed and bound in Great Britain by
Collins, Glasgow

HEADLINE BOOK PUBLISHING PLC
Headline House
79 Great Titchfield Street
London W1P 7FN

For Ben Hudson,
magician and friend

One

Channing Stuart had been seven years old before she realized there were people in the world who didn't earn their living by magic. Now, a quarter of a century later, sliding noiselessly through a door in the backstage area of a Los Angeles nightclub, she smelled the familiar aroma of a magician's dressing rooms, a combination of glycerin and zinc stearate, and hovered briefly on the edge of something like homesickness.

The old man standing with his back to her methodically checked the endless secret pockets of his black suit. He was stout and white-haired.

"Hey, Yussuf," she said. "Bet you can't do this one!"

Yussuf whirled. She must really have gotten him this time, she thought. She'd never seen him jump like that.

"Channing!" he gasped.

Relishing the moment, she extended a long-fingered hand, wearing a small, dark ruby and sprinkled with the freckles that ran all the way to her shoulders. It poised a second, and then the fingers flicked imperceptibly. Silver coins appeared between them—out of thin air, it seemed. She caught the coins, squeezed them, spread her palm to display emptiness. She squeezed again and displayed the coins strung in a bracelet. Perfecting the trick had filled the long nights of the six months when she'd been drilling for water in the United Arab Emirates. She grinned now, pleased with her own cleverness.

"Channing!" Yussuf repeated. He came toward her like one in a trance, gripping the shoulders of the long, black, sequin-trimmed dress that helped her accomplish some of her magic, and brushed a kiss on her cheek. "I can't believe it!"

The last time he'd surprised her, she'd been in Bolivia, grappling with the problems of digging wells in soil that was compacted. She returned his hug.

"Oh, Yussuf, I'm sorry to get here when the show's already started. I'd forgotten about L.A. traffic. I'll go out front and watch—"

"No! Wait." He released her, looking oddly tense. "You've got to help me! I go on in"—he glanced at a clock on the wall—"eight minutes. And look." He held up his hands. "Arthritis. It hit this morning. It's always gone in a few days, but right now I can hardly fan cards. I was standing here just now wondering how I'd ever do close-up."

The delight she'd felt at surprising him started to lose its edge. She hadn't expected to see age catching up with Yussuf, though of course she should have known it would. He'd been her grandfather's friend. She'd known him all her thirty-two years. Yet an old wound made her hesitate at what he was asking.

"Please!" He sounded desperate, and she'd never heard that note in his voice before. "All you'd have to do is . . . how about what you pulled on me that time in Cairo? We'd get a few laughs."

"Cairo, huh?"

She began to chuckle as she remembered. Her work in groundwater geology took her all over the world, and whenever one of Yussuf's bookings brought them within a few hundred miles of each other, they got together. They were both without family. The tie between them was the only one either had left.

With one hand she smoothed back hair the color of cinnamon. Wasn't she a Stuart, once destined to become the fourth in a line of professional magicians? When other little girls had been taking dancing lessons, she'd been perfecting the oblique palm.

Then she'd turned her back on that world.

No matter. She could still help Yussuf.

"Just get into the audience," he was saying as he took her elbow. "There's a house table, and it's empty tonight. Sit there." He checked the clock again.

Outside, beneath the dressing room window, something made a soft thump. They both turned.

"Wind," said Yussuf. He seemed to hover indecisively for a moment, then moved abruptly back toward his street clothes on their brass hook. "Here." He thrust his arm into a pocket and handed her a cassette tape. "I was going to send you this. Instructions for my upside-down king trick you never could figure out."

A sadness began to envelop Channing. Yussuf must feel his days of performing were numbered if he was giving her the secret of a trick he'd never shared with anyone. It was how magic passed from generation to generation. Only, she felt unworthy —outside the fraternity.

As Yussuf opened the door she noticed slacks and a black turtleneck spread on a nearby couch. Child's clothes, they looked like, with sales tags still attached.

She'd ask about them later. Right now Yussuf had her elbow.

"Now listen," he was saying. "You'll come after the doves."

Outside, the gun with the silencer eased back from the magician's window. Too late. Too late by seconds. The man who held it cursed.

And now there was another complication. Yussuf Bashim had passed something to the woman. A tape, it looked like. Names. Plans. Enough to ruin everything, maybe. The magician was trying to cut himself into the deal with blackmail, so it was a safe bet.

Very well, he would take care of the magician and then the woman. His hand reached for the windowsill.

From the other end of the darkened alley his experienced ears caught a sound. He froze, swinging by habit into a crouching position, his gun at the ready. Two eddies disturbed the smooth flow of darkness. There. Against the wall. He waited.

The alley wall scraped Bill Ellery's back as he and his partner edged along it.

"Sure he turned in here?" whispered Sam Brown,

the hand that held his snub-nosed Chief's Special just brushing Ellery's jacket.

"Yeah. I'm sure."

Henri Ballieu, terrorist wanted for murder in half a dozen countries, known for shooting his victims through the throat so they couldn't talk before they died, was theirs for the taking. Ellery wondered vaguely how, with the FBI, Interpol, and Immigration watching for the man, he'd still slipped by. There'd be grumbling from the brass if he and Sam had to use their weapons; the U.S. State Department like its special agents to keep a low profile. But he'd read and reread Ballieu's dossier and doubted they could just walk up and hand the man an engraved invitation to a prison cell with color TV.

"Man, you were right," breathed Sammy, his black skin lost in the darkness. "Lord knows how fresh in the country—hours, maybe—and coming right to old friend Yussuf! Makes cramping my knees in that bar across the street almost worth it. How d'you figure these things?"

Now wasn't the time to chat about logic. The hunch that had kept them staking out this area since late afternoon had finally paid off.

"Let's take him alive," said Ellery. "Need to find out who has that film."

If they blew this, Ballieu might get what he was after, the stolen piece of film needed to make official U.S. passports. Ballieu and his group would churn out good copies, provide them to any malcontents that met their price. Where they'd had to sneak into a country before, they'd walk in brazenly, through

Immigration. Terrorism would spread like venereal disease.

Ellery began to move again but cautiously, ears straining. As a teenager he had despised the spare and only average-size frame that kept him from the football and basketball teams where his older brother had cut the usual shining path. In a situation like this, though, it seemed preferable to Sam's solid quarterback shape. Deliberately he relaxed the fingers curving around his .38. A looser grip, a smoother shot.

He never saw the movement, only the fire flash of a gun in the instant before Sammy's strangled cry. Sammy crumpled beside him.

Ellery dove in another direction, firing as he went —two shots. Something stung his shoulder.

A light came on, flooding the alley with pale visibility. No sign of anyone; sounds of running. He stumbled to his feet, pausing over Sammy.

"Sam! Sammy . . . ?"

The man who had been his partner and friend for four years had been shot through the jugular vein. The bastard had killed him. Ellery felt something warm seeping down under his own jacket. No time to check it now. He had a job to do.

A back door to the nightclub was opening. No doubt drawn by the sound of gunfire, a couple of stagehands ran out.

"Call an ambulance!" Ellery shouted. "There's a federal officer down back here!"

He knew it was too late for Sammy, but he could hope against hope. He took off running, zigzagging, dodging into the shelter of garbage cans.

By the time he reached the sidewalk at the end of the alley, he knew it was no good. His mouth tightened into a line of grimness beyond his thirty-nine years. This job was the only thing that had ever made sense to him. The only thing he'd ever been good at. And now he'd blown one. He'd lost Sammy; lost his quarry too.

Where had Ballieu gone? Ellery stopped for breath. His arm was bleeding. More than he'd thought at first. Now he became aware of scalding pain as well. He peeled off his jacket, yanked his tie into a tourniquet to stop the worst of the flow, and tried to think.

Overhead, the marquee above the door of the club he and Sam had watched all afternoon blinked on and off: THE WORLD-FAMOUS MAGIC OF YUSSUF.

Inside. Maybe Ballieu had slipped inside, melted into the crowd. It was his style, covering himself with innocent people. It took a certain amount of guts, Ellery supposed, but it sure as hell was effective.

Stuffing his .38 back into its holster and shrugging his jacket on to cover his blood-soaked sleeve, he opened the door. He felt a momentary surge of dizziness. Ought to call for help, but this was going down too fast.

He hoped he wasn't going to faint.

Channing sat at the front-row table with the RESERVED sign on it and checked her cuff links one final time. Onstage, Yussuf was opening his act with a dazzling display of the Chinese linking rings.

Her fingertips traced the cuff links. They were

gold, like the case of her *kunjar,* the small, J-shaped Arabic knife that hung at her waist. Gifts from two different worlds, she thought. The *kunjar* had been given her by a friend, a sultan's daughter. Channing wore it as an ornament, an exquisitely carved piece of jewelry—though in a pinch she knew it could serve its intended purpose as well. The cuff links she wore because they'd been a gift from Gramps, before their differences.

She closed her eyes, determined not to reflect on the choice she'd made.

Never look back. That was her motto.

Still, she felt the irony of sitting here helping Yussuf. She felt the irony of being in shape to help because for ten years she'd practiced nightly with no audience other than camels or elephants or occasionally a few curious members of her crew too bored for a poker game.

She accomplished something in the work she did —reducing disease, adding years to the lives of women who would have grown old carrying water —and after Tony's death, accomplishing something had seemed even more important. Yet the need to do magic remained in her blood like a hunger, an addiction.

She focused on the stage. Yussuf was draping a square of red silk over an empty drinking glass. It was almost time. He whisked the scarf away and four doves flew out over the audience.

Oohs and ahhhs erupted everywhere, then enthusiastic applause. Channing turned to watch the birds make their way to a handler, and noticed a man standing at the back of the room, one shoulder drawn up. Odd, him standing when there were a few tables empty. He seemed to be looking for someone. She didn't know why she had noticed him. The chin, maybe.

She drew her attention back, aware of Yussuf in the audience now, beginning what would be his greatly abbreviated close-up routine.

"And now some little puzzlements with cards," he was saying. "After all, what's a bird in a glass compared with an ace up your sleeve?"

As he spoke, he reached toward a middle-aged woman whose basketball-size bosoms were cantilevered out beneath a pink spangled dress. He pulled a large silk scarf emblazoned with the ace of clubs from one of her brief cap sleeves. The audience roared.

He did another simple trick, finally making his way to Channing's table.

"You'd like to help me, wouldn't you, young lady?" he boomed. "Just pick a card . . . don't tell me which one . . ."

He gave a tiny wink, then held them out.

Like a bolt, Channing felt the sudden joy of performing, the thought that the mysteries accomplished by her fingers had been passed down through countless conjurers through countless ages, and that still in this age of science and microseconds the hand was quicker than the eye.

"I think I'll take this one," she said, reaching toward Yussuf's head and, with a turn of the wrist, producing a card from his left ear. "Or maybe one of these." She pulled three cards from his right ear, one after the other. Observers at nearby tables started to laugh.

"You seem to have cards in the strangest places," she said, teasing, as she let her skilled fingers seem to pluck them from his head, his collar, his pockets.

Yussuf pretended to be mortified, his hands chasing and slapping at hers. This was how she had turned the tables on him in Cairo when he'd spotted her in the audience—though of course he hadn't expected this then. The audience was loving it. Channing grinned. She felt like such a ham when she performed, and like it should all be harder, somehow.

"You know, I really think it would be much more interesting if you did something useful—like filling my hand with silver," she said to Yussuf.

"You want that?" He gave a wonderful imitation of an indignant shout. "All right. Hold out your hand!"

Channing complied, suspending her hand in air just long enough to be sure of good attention before flexing muscles and spinning into the new trick she'd learned for Yussuf: Empty fingers. Coins. Hand closed and open again. Coins gone.

The applause began before she was even halfway done. They realized now that she was part of the act. Yussuf beamed, took her hand, and bowed to her. Channing smiled up at him, and it was in that instant she saw his own smile fade. His eyes fixed on something. His arm moved. She heard a soft pop.

In the first long seconds she didn't understand. Then Yussuf's body came crashing down onto her table. His hand was clutching his throat, and red seeped out of it. People were screaming. She sat paralyzed. She heard herself call Yussuf's name. Memory flashed her back to a restaurant in Beirut. Blood. Pandemonium. The knowledge in her stomach that Tony was dead. The horrible knowledge that because she had stopped to look in a shop and was five minutes late, she was alive.

She pressed her palms against the reality of the table and looked up in shock.

People were moving. The man she'd noticed standing in the back of the room was zigzagging through the tables, a gun in his hand. He leapt to the stage.

"Everybody sit still!"

The way he'd run, the way he was looking around with gun at the ready, made her realize he wasn't the one who'd shot Yussuf. Her numbness was starting to leave, and she cast a confirming look at the old man slumped before her. He was motionless. His eyes were bulging.

And then she saw it, lying next to Yussuf's splayed fingers.

A tiny handgun.

Why? Why was Yussuf carrying it? For innocent reasons, surely. The man on the stage was swinging around, looking at Yussuf. Would he spot the gun?

"Mr. Yussuf! Mr. Yussuf!"

The boy's voice broke through the heavy motions of her brain. He was twelve or thereabouts, Hispanic, dressed in tatters. She didn't know where he'd come from, but he hurtled forward, throwing himself on Yussuf's body. Sobs tore fiercely from his slender form.

"You were going to teach me to be a magician! You promised!"

Channing heard in his words a loneliness, a sense of loss that matched her own. Instinctively she reached out to circle him with her arm. As she did, her right hand, almost with a mind of its own, moved independently. The nimbleness of her fingers was slowed by the unfamiliar shape of the gun. It was crazy trying to make vanish an object she'd never worked with. But she'd known Yussuf all her life.

Her hand hadn't paused, had continued its arc toward the boy's other shoulder, but the gun was in her sleeve now. Channing looked up nervously. The man on the stage—whoever he was—was staring at her. Had he seen?

Two

The detective was loud and arrogant and sucked his sinuses dry to punctuate his sentences. He had shoved the boy, who was still fighting sobs, onto the couch in Yussuf's dressing room and was yelling at him.

"Hey. He should have his parents here if you want to question him," Channing said angrily.

With a great clearing of his nasal passages the behemoth swung on her.

"You want a lawyer, you get one, lady. 'Cause I got some questions for you."

Behind the detective, dwarfed by him, the boy looked frightened. His eyes were somber beyond his years, and his collarbone stood out under a shirt meant for someone larger. Channing couldn't stand hunger, couldn't stand suffering; it was why she'd chosen the work she had—to fight it. Her heart reached out to the boy.

"A witness says the magician pulled a gun," the detective said. "What happened to it?"

Channing looked at him levelly.

"People think they see a lot of things—especially in crowd situations." The words just tumbled out. "It's a phenomenon well known by illusionists. I never saw anything."

She'd felt she owed it to Yussuf to hide the gun.

There was probably some perfectly logical explanation for it. He'd gotten used to carrying one because of so much travel, maybe. If the press learned about it, though, there'd be innuendos. She wasn't going to let that happen to Yussuf's name. Not just to help this vacuum-nose, she wasn't.

He glared at her and she relaxed deliberately. Her gaze was clear to telegraph her confidence. She savored his moment of recognition as angry red suffused his face. It wasn't the first time some overbearing official had realized he couldn't budge her; she'd run some real gauntlets getting drilling permits in foreign countries.

The detective grilled her with a few more questions, then turned back to the boy. After a few minutes he flipped his notebook shut in disgust.

"Go on. Both of you."

They walked out together, neither speaking. As they reached the street the boy, whose name was Serafin, hunched his shoulders.

In a flash, and because she was watching him, Channing recognized the gesture. She knew that wary glide of a gaze up the street. She'd seen that look on children sleeping in doorways, on children clamoring to watch her jeep for a few baht or piasters in some foreign city.

He had nowhere to go. His grief over losing Yussuf must be as great as her own—even worse, considering his age. She heard him swallow a dry sob. He didn't look as though he'd had a meal in a week.

"You lied about where you lived. You don't live anywhere, do you?"

She wondered why she had to work to keep her voice from shaking.

He squinted at her. His legs were preparing for flight.

"My mom moves a lot."

"Uh-huh."

In the instant he leapt from the steps, Channing jerked him back by the waist of his pants.

"Listen, if I have to turn you in to Children's Services, neither one of us will get any sleep tonight. It would be a lot simpler if you came home with me. Yussuf came to my house a lot."

Still wiggling, he looked at her in surprise.

Well, now I've done it, Channing thought. There were probably laws against this. But she knew he must feel lost and sick at heart tonight. So did she. It seemed right for them to be together. She was sure those clothes on Yussuf's couch had been for the boy. It seemed right to do something for him.

Besides, she'd always felt slightly guilty about all the unused space in the big house she'd inherited in Altadena.

"You've lost a lot of blood, Mr. Ellery. We're going to admit you."

"Jesus Christ, *no*!"

Bill Ellery came to with a start. He'd been trying to figure where Ballieu might go, letting them fix his shoulder. Now a childhood panic hit him in the gut. He struggled to sit.

A rubber tube jerked him back. He was in a curtained-off cubicle of the emergency room. They had some kind of IV hooked to him. Trapping him, like before.

He'd been eleven then, left alone for a week in a foreign hospital where he couldn't speak the language. His leg in traction. Vomiting and having to lie in the mess because he couldn't move. A huge nurse slapping him. Helpless. And worst of all . . .

"You said the bullet was out—a clean wound."

He fought his irrational fear, ashamed at his loss of control. So much for hitching a ride with the local police to get to the hospital, he thought.

The doctor, a woman, was frowning over a chart. "It *is* out—and you've lost three pints of blood."

"Yeah, well. I've always been careless."

He tried to grin.

His parents had left him in that Swiss hospital because he hadn't met their specifications—too average in school, too inward and tongue-tied, an annoyance to them, unlike his brother, Reid. Yet maybe it was lying there, scared shitless, that had taught him grit, he thought. Grit was the one thing he had in abundance.

Not the zeal to make a million bucks before he was thirty, as his father had done. Not the knack for trite conversation that might have pleased his mother. Not Reid's thirst for power. The rest of the family thought he was a poet, a dropout, an underachiever. It gave him a perverse satisfaction.

"We need to observe you for twenty-four hours," the doctor said crisply.

Ellery shook his head, dislodging a cowlick of brown hair.

The State Department needed him. Was depending on him. And a long time ago he'd come to see how much difference one man could make in the world. He'd been working the film case since it had popped ten days ago. He owed it to the department to see things through—to Sammy, too, he thought grimly.

Sam had promised his oldest a ten-speed for Christmas. Ellery made a mental note to make sure that happened.

"Could I have my shirt?"

He raised himself on an elbow that wobbled. A nurse was appraising his naked torso with undisguised interest. The doctor, making notes on a chart, flicked a look at him.

"Who's your next of kin, Mr. Ellery?"

Jesus Christ, did he have to promise he'd eat liver three meals a day?

"No next of kin. I'm in town on business." He held his impatience, made the words sound reasonable.

Henri Ballieu was out there somewhere, waiting for that film, and he was going to see Ballieu didn't get it. Last year Ballieu's group had blown up a department store full of people. Six months ago they'd kidnapped and killed a woman with kids just because her father happened to be a politician. If they got the capacity to make U.S. passports, they'd be turning up everywhere.

As a kid, Ellery had daydreamed a lot. He'd wondered how you insured justice and freedom and all the other things no one else around him seemed to talk, or even think, about. Even in three years of law school not many people talked about them. They seemed too intangible. Too elusive, maybe. But in his work, he'd come to learn some of the answers.

"Unhook me, will you?"

He swung his legs over the edge of the gurney that held him.

The nurse and an intern looked nervous. They'd seen his identification, he guessed. Or his gun.

The frosty little doctor gave a jerk of her head, and the intern reached for a hypodermic needle. Oh, Christ. They'd sedated him when he'd been that scared little kid too. He could feel a cold sweat starting.

Then a deep voice barked on the other side of the curtains.

"I don't care where I'm supposed to be. You treating a man who was shot in the shoulder?"

Bill Ellery's fists unclenched at the familiar voice. He knew with relief that he'd get out of there. He wouldn't have to lie awake, tense, stalked by the memory of the orderly in that expensive hospital all those years ago who had tried to sodomize him.

Grinning at the doctor, who didn't seem to be taking defeat very well, he reminded himself to tell his boss about that girl in black who'd made the magician's gun disappear.

The house in Altadena was white and two stories high and captured the graciousness of a bygone era. Channing's parents had died in an accident when she was five, and she had grown up here. She couldn't bring herself to part with the house. Maintaining it seemed the most fitting memorial possible to the couple who'd reared her. In this house her grandfather, The Great Sebastian, had held her on his knee and taught her magic tricks from the time her fingers could hold cards. In this house her grandmother, a diminutive New England lady as fragile and strong as fine porcelain, had fed a constant stream of less successful magicians and set a daily example of tolerance for those around her.

Serafin looked at the house and shook his head. Channing guessed he was thinking of money. Gramps had left some. Her own income was good. She'd made wise investments. There wasn't any problem maintaining the house.

An elderly houseman, features puckered as though he'd been sucking limes, met them as the door opened. Channing had inherited him from her grandfather too. Or so it seemed to her. He was caretaker in her absence, critic when she was present.

"Now what?" he demanded, peering along the bridge of his hooked nose at Serafin.

Channing tossed her evening bag toward a table. "This is Serafin. Get him something to eat and show him a room. Yussuf was shot tonight. He's dead."

She saw a kaleidoscope of emotions across Rundell's face. He was shocked by the news about Yussuf, who had come here often; he was at an utter loss confronting a child. His expression settled quickly into a practiced glare of disapproval.

Rundell disapproved of almost anything she did. Even now, jangled as she was, Channing loved his predictability. He'd been part of the household ever since she could remember, and it had seemed unconscionable to separate him and the house—another reason for not selling. At his age, with his disposition, he'd never find another job. And he'd wither away without someone to harp at. Knowing full well she wouldn't escape his grilling for long, Channing climbed the curved central staircase to the room she'd occupied since she was a child.

Closing the door, she leaned against it and let out her breath. She was tired—more tired from yesterday's long trip home than she'd realized. Abu Dhabi to Riyadh. Riyadh to Paris. Finally the transatlantic flight, and the last leg, New York to California.

Action. Action was the key to keeping your mind from troubling thoughts. Pushing herself briskly from the door, discarding her *kunjar,* she let her black magician's dress slide to the floor. She spread its folds out over the back of a chair. She would hang it tomorrow.

Why had someone killed Yussuf?

A sense of anger and loss pushed through in spite of her efforts. Yussuf had been an old man, a magician, his very life devoted to making people happy.

She winced a little from the thought.

Ten years ago that hadn't seemed enough to her. She'd wanted to make the world better. Gramps couldn't understand. He'd never grasped how deeply their trip to Egypt the year she was sixteen had affected her. That terrible village. People starving because there was no way of growing food. Babies dying from dehydration. And out in the desert, the signs of water coming, but not fast enough for most of those people.

Science had always been easy for her. She'd decided then, at sixteen. But Gramps hadn't taken her seriously, not even when she got her degree in hydro-geology. Not until she'd told him she'd been approved for a graduate program abroad and she was accepting.

She'd tried to make him understand that she loved magic, but that she somehow had to give a better accounting of her life. After all, she'd survived the accident that killed her parents. Shouldn't one Stuart out of four generations do something besides entertain?

He'd raged, yelled bitterly that she wasn't a Stuart. It felt like a curse. In the end she'd gone off, anyway, and two weeks later Gramps was dead.

Yussuf had been en route to an engagement and had brought the news to her. It had been the start of the visits and the tricks they played on each other. In a way they'd never known each other well, yet there'd been a bond.

Action.

She outraced the emotions that wanted to claim her, drew on a white silk robe, and went downstairs.

The living room still bore her grandmother's imprint. Good quality seascapes hung on the walls. A sofa and chairs were upholstered in moss-green velvet. A writing desk and other pieces in the comfortable room were authentic Sheraton.

It was a room that soothed Channing. She sat down in a wing chair. Picking up a quarter, she let it dance back and forth across the backs of her fingers. That act also steadied her.

A footstep sounded. Rundell padded in at a majestic totter.

"This isn't some sheikhdom, madam," he began severely.

He'd started calling her madam the day she'd signed his first paycheck. This opening was one of his favorites. It led to a lecture on rashness, and Channing realized if he'd omitted it, she'd have been disappointed. She grinned in spite of herself.

"How's Serafin?"

"Splendid—but you can't afford to feed him." Rundell's teeth clicked shut. Subject closed. He grunted as he bent to turn on a lamp. "Where did you find him?"

"He was hanging around to see Yussuf. He didn't have a place—"

"I'll make a nightcap. You can start at the beginning," he said, interrupting.

Channing wondered briefly how they'd ever come to this ritual. She really wasn't fond of liquor late in the evening. Rundell was—and she supposed he liked to feel that he was coddling her.

"Make one for both of us," she said. That was part of the ritual, too, the urging. You had to make allowances if you wanted to keep an adversary as good as Rundell.

As he splashed whiskey and soda into glasses she summarized her visit with Yussuf and all that had happened afterward. Feeling as though she'd been in a nightmare, Channing brushed a hand across her eyes.

"God. I stole a gun, too . . . Police evidence."

"I suppose you want me to put it down the garbage disposal?" Rundell said sourly. He clunked her glass down beside her and lowered himself to a chair facing hers. "Madam, you're—"

"Impulsive, spoiled, hardheaded, and too old to behave like a tomboy. Did I forget anything?"

Rundell hated it when she stole his thunder. She heard him sniff.

"Sloppy. You drop your clothes everywhere." He knocked back half his drink. "I wish you'd find a man to tumble around with. You'd be a hell of a lot less trouble."

Her passport said Annette Lewis, but her real name was Khadija. Her hair was black. Her lips were full, alluring in their sultry discontent as she stood in the customs line. Inside the lining of the sable coat slung over her shoulders she carried two million dollars. Inside her belt she wore enough plastic explosive to destroy herself and the money, should it be discovered.

The man at the customs gate closed her suitcase. She was in Los Angeles.

She moved toward the taxi area, smiling at the stupid American pigs who tried to flirt with her. Bringing in the money Ballieu needed had been her responsibility. She had volunteered for the job. Volunteered because she wanted to meet Henri Ballieu.

He was an old man, almost fifty. Too old for this job, too cautious, the younger members of the cell in Paris said.

Khadija flexed lithe muscles, their deadly skills hidden beneath the tight jeans and expensive capitalist whore boots that her mission required as disguise. She was here to advance herself, to report any flaw in Ballieu's judgment—and to make sure nothing went wrong.

She slung her coat into the back of a taxi that opened its door to her.

Though no one knew it, she had a personal reason for wanting to cause the downfall of Henri Ballieu.

Near a boarded-up fish house in Topanga Canyon, Ballieu stepped out of a phone booth. Pain twisted his belly. Three years ago they'd said they'd cut the pain out of him, but they hadn't.

It was why he was going to get this piece of film at any cost—as a memorial to himself. And nobody knew. His pale eyes scanned the twisting two-lane road that led through the canyon. It was almost deserted at this hour. His car, left where it was expected by American comrades, was hidden in shadows. He was satisfied he hadn't been followed.

Ballieu smoothed back thinning blond hair, the legacy of his French father. It had been an easy matter to call the still frantic nightclub, say he wanted to book the girl who had helped with the magic act, get her name and telephone number. Tomorrow it would be equally easy to get rid of her.

He started toward his car, reflexes quickening as another car pulled off and stopped. A youth in shorts and a sweatshirt got out and started toward the telephone booth. He glanced at Ballieu. Innocent, probably, but Henri Ballieu didn't believe in taking risks.

"Excuse me," Ballieu said. "I'm trying to find a friend's house."

Americans were so fawningly accommodating. Ballieu plunged his knife in as the youth turned.

The knife was better than using a bullet, which could be linked and identified. As soon as the death shudder came, Ballieu pulled on surgical gloves. He picked money out of the dead man's wallet to make it look like robbery and extracted the knife.

Judgment, he thought with a vicious triumph. Judgment was what gave him an edge. There were those who thought he was growing too old for his work, but he would show them. He had taken care of the greedy magician. He had lost the men in the alley. In little more than forty-eight hours he could get the film.

The single problem remaining was the woman who had received that cassette tape.

Ballieu wiped his knife on his victim's sweatshirt and, with his tongue, absently licked away a warm stain that remained at the hilt.

Three

Bill Ellery rolled over and felt the fire dart in jagged bolts through his shoulder. He opened his eyes on a standard hotel clock-radio. Eight o'clock. When had he ever slept until eight in the midst of a crisis? Why had Oliver let him?

He swung his hips from the bed and sat for a moment, clad only in narrow white briefs. Good old basic Bill, he thought bitterly. No colored jocks, no after-shave, because your brother, the smart young senator, always chose both so carefully.

A lot of good the basics had done him last night. He'd still lost Sammy. His throat knotted so he could hardly swallow. He remembered that feeling. It was how you held in tears.

Sammy had been the first real friend he'd ever had. He'd understood Ellery's sense of humor. They'd talked about things—all kinds of things. Sam's family had begged Ellery to join them for holidays, something his own parents, as they Christmased in Vail and summered at Lyford Cay, had never done. Ellery had found a secondhand boat like Sam had always wanted and made a little payment on the side so the price came down to what Sam, with a family to feed, could afford.

Sam was the gentlest and most decent man he'd

ever known. They'd been partners for almost four years.

Ellery shook his head. Must be the pain pills they'd given him in the emergency room that were making him entertain such random thoughts. Through the door to a connecting sitting room he could see the steel-gray hair and straight back of Oliver Lemming, director of special projects, his boss. On the phone already in their makeshift command post, and had probably been up all night. Going into the bathroom, Ellery scrubbed his face to alertness, combed back the healthy mop of hair he noticed again was getting too long, then made his way into the sitting room, fastening his slacks.

"How you feeling?" Oliver turned at the first hint of sound. He was small and trim, plainspoken. Once an agent himself, he understood better than most the delicate balance between practicality and bureaucracy. Ellery liked him.

"I'll make it," he said, easing onto a couch.

Oliver pointed to coffee.

"Have some. Hope you don't mind my bunking where Sam was. It made most sense under the circumstances."

Ellery nodded. One of the things he admired in Oliver was the man's sensitivity. Even faced with the need for expediency, Oliver didn't overlook the fact that a man had lost his life, didn't step in as though they were all interchangeable parts.

The older man stood up to straighten his back, wincing a little. He looked worn, and his face was showing a stubble of beard. The phone beside several legal pads filled with scribbling rang again. Oliver held a brief conversation.

"Shouldn't have let me sleep so long," said Ellery when he'd hung up. "You get any yourself?"

"Couple of hours." Oliver grimaced again, still rubbing his spine. "Haven't learned a lot. Ballieu's dropped from sight. I figured no point us both losing sleep." His shaggy eyebrows drew together. "We're in a real mess here. I'd feel better if you'd checked into the hospital with that shoulder, but I'm damn glad you didn't."

The compliment did more good than painkillers for Bill Ellery. He took a long slug of coffee. Compliments were something he'd never had many of while growing up.

"What'd you find out about the girl?"

In spite of weariness, Oliver's eyes gave a twinkle. "No wonder you don't have a love life, son. They like to be called women these days. Anyway, she's thirty-two."

He drew a breath, and Ellery knew that whatever came next wasn't going to be to his liking and that Oliver knew it.

"Bill. I think we can use her for bait. To catch Ballieu."

The older man raised a hand to silence his protest.

"I know. You saw her make Yussuf's gun disappear. You told the police and they asked, and she told them she never saw a gun. I still think she's clean."

Ellery could feel his jaw hardening. Barely ten days had passed since two government couriers on their way to the engraving office in Washington had been ambushed and killed, the passport film they were transporting stolen. Through Interpol, which had an informer, State had learned Yussuf had set up the sale of the film. He was the go-between. And Oliver wanted to trust the girl who'd been with him the night before?

The gray-haired former agent sank into a chair across from him.

"You saw for yourself, she's good at sleight of hand," said Oliver. "Fourth-generation magician, or would have been if she'd turned professional, I understand. She's traveled a lot. . . ."

Ellery was deciphering scribbles on the yellow legal pad in Oliver's hand. Notes on Channing Stuart. U.N. clearance. Ph.D. in hydro-geology—why the hell would a woman study something like that? It intrigued him. There was a list of countries she'd worked in . . . people who knew her. Oliver had clearly put in a long night tracking this down. He was speaking again.

"Bill. She could convince Ballieu she's taken over Yussuf's network. She could go to that meeting. She could get close enough to do sleight of hand on that film, substitute a piece that's imperceptibly flawed for the real thing. We'd be able to spot anyone who used one of their phony passports. Police in a dozen countries could lock up would-be hijackers, potential kidnappers—"

"Holy Christ, Oliver! Have you been sniffing talc or something?"

"I'm dead serious. We know when and where Ballieu's to pick up that film. We don't know who has it.

Even if we find out, we'd only have two fish. This way we could catch a whole freezer full."

Already Ellery was on his feet and pacing.

"Uh-uh." He saw where this was leading. "Clean or not, the girl's an amateur, Oliver. I don't want her blood on my hands—and the plan's crazy."

"You're the only one I'd trust. You're the best we have."

Ellery shook his head stubbornly. He wasn't falling for flattery. If Channing Stuart was honest, then she must also be naive. She might be smart, but she wasn't a match for someone like Ballieu. He already had Sam on his conscience. He could feel the man who had been his mentor studying him.

"What happened to Sam wasn't your fault." The director's voice sharpened. He sucked irritably on a pipe he'd produced from his pocket. "You don't have a choice. It's an order."

Ellery turned, mouth hardening. He wasn't used to the pulling of rank.

"Get your jacket," his boss said, easing back. "We'll grab breakfast somewhere."

Ellery held his irritation for another moment, then let it go.

"Great. Know a place that serves liver?"

Aware a truce had been offered, Oliver shook his head in perplexity.

"You have the damnedest sense of humor. Come on. We'll eat, then touch base with the boys at FBI. After that I want to head up to Altadena to visit the lady with the fancy fingers."

* * *

"You going to send me back to Mexico like they did my folks?"

Channing, leaning against the mantelpiece in her breakfast room and watching the boy who had just spoken shovel more eggs and bacon into his mouth, fought an urge to laugh. Why spoil her perfect record of irrational acts since Yussuf's death?

First she'd palmed the gun. Then she'd brought Serafin here. Now she discovered she was harboring an illegal alien in her sunny breakfast room. His parents had been caught and sent back twice. His mother had been near death with cancer, anyway, he'd told her this morning. Serafin had eluded the authorities. He wanted to stay.

Rundell, shoulders stooping, came in to slam a pot of jam on the table.

"You'll get yourself in trouble," he hissed.

Channing hadn't requested jam. The irascible houseman no doubt had had his ear pressed against the other side of the swinging door.

As Rundell stalked out again, Channing wondered if she should blame her recent behavior on premature senility. Or perhaps on the fact that she'd lived too long away from civilization, drawing guidance from her own judgment where laws were few. There was, of course, the possibility of plain strong-headedness.

"*Are* you going to send me back?" demanded Serafin. His voice had a wobble that he tried to hide.

Channing checked the coffee cup sitting beside her on the mantel. It was empty.

"I don't know . . . no. Of course I'm not going to send you back."

She had money, didn't she? She wasn't exactly the mothering type, but they'd get along. How could she turn her back on such a determined and obviously self-possessed kid?

"Why'd you hide Yussuf's gun?"

Her fingers raked the hair at her temples as she sought an answer.

"Impulse, I guess. Goodness knows what the newspapers would have made of a gun—you know how they are."

Serafin was a darkly handsome boy, his eyes unnervingly wise. They followed her gravely as she came toward the table to refill her coffee cup.

"You don't know any trouble Yussuf was having?" she said, prodding. "No arguments or anything?"

What weighed on her mind this morning was why anyone would shoot her friend. When she'd asked the police the previous night, they'd shrugged it off—the city was full of nuts.

Serafin shook his head.

"He said he was going to retire after his next booking. He said he might take me with him."

The news saddened her. Yussuf's arthritis, she guessed. What was a magician without his hands? If they'd had time to talk, if she and Yussuf had gone to dinner as they usually did, she supposed he'd have told her his plans.

Her thoughts were stopped by the *whoosh* of the swinging door. Rundell reappeared, in his official mode now.

"Two gentlemen to see you, madam. They *say* they're from the State Department."

The announcement derailed Channing completely. The police she could understand, but the State Department? It couldn't be about Serafin. Too fast. And they wouldn't know he was here. What else could it be?

The way she'd dealt with that fat *shaykh* who'd tried to force himself on her last night in the UAE? If complaints were lodged against her, there was always the chance she'd lose her clearance for working in countries where diplomacy was needed. What else could go wrong?

"I'll see them in the study," she said, and began to move briskly. Nine times out of ten you could circumvent trouble with a good offense.

The study that had been her grandfather's was on the second floor and was the room in the house where Channing, away for such blocks of time now, felt most at home. As a child she'd spent countless hours here, sitting on the massive desk or on her grandfather's lap, watching, learning, practicing. She slipped behind the desk and waited, standing, as Rundell showed the two men in. The one with silver hair held out his hand.

"Dr. Stuart? I'm Oliver Lemming. This is my associate, William Ellery."

The second man was in his late thirties. His mouth was hard, with a hint of underlying humor that might be too biting for some people, Channing suspected. But that was irrelevant.

"I suppose you're here because of the swing I took at that lecherous old Shaykh Omar," she began. "Well let me tell you, I had every right! I had witnesses, and it's well known he's harassed other foreign women—"

"Dr. Stuart." Lemming's voice showed signs of weariness as he cut in. "We're not here to make trouble. We don't know a thing about Shaykh Omar. We're here to ask your help. May we sit down?"

Puzzled now but still wary, she gestured toward chairs. Lemming sank into one in front of her desk, but Bill Ellery strolled toward the window. He eyed the life-size portrait of her grandfather on one wall; her grandfather's folded cape, his wand, and top hat on a chest that was really a sword cabinet. Slouching slightly against the window, he turned to eye her carefully too. Daylight through the glass behind him highlighted glints of black and red in his brown hair. He didn't like her.

That was all right with Channing. Men, particularly those quite sure of themselves, often didn't like her on first meeting. Bringing them around was fun. If she chose to do it.

Oliver Lemming was speaking.

"Dr. Stuart, Bill here says Yussuf Bashim had a gun last night and that you made it disappear."

Damn. Now she recognized him. The man on the stage.

Bill Ellery watched her weigh and decide her answer, all in a split second. She had freckles up to the rolled sleeves of her white shirt and across the bridge of her nose. An assertive chin. Quarrelsome.

"All right," she said. "I did it. I know it was dumb. But I'd known Yussuf all my life. I couldn't stand the thought of seeing his name dragged—"

"How much did you know about his business?" Ellery cut in abruptly.

He could see her brain turning, trying to figure this out. He hadn't made much time in his life for women—relax too much and he might not be as good at the job as he ought to be. Still, this one struck him as different.

"What he earned? Who handled his bookings, you mean?" she asked. "Not much."

If she was clean—and he was starting to think Oliver was right on that point—she'd never stand a chance in the role carved out for her. She was fast, he'd give her that. But too much of her thought process showed; it would be a giveaway.

"What about contacts in other countries?" he said, pressing on.

She shook her head. "What does the State Department—"

Channing was starting to feel uneasy, but before she could finish her question, the man in front of her desk spoke again.

"Ms. Stuart, we don't have time to be nice about this. Your friend Yussuf was as crooked as they come. In the past five years he'd set himself up quite a network, supplying things to various terrorist groups around the world—weapons, explosives, counterfeit currency, you name it."

The arms of her chair felt cold and unfamiliar as Channing groped for them.

"You can't be right! He was—"

"We have photographs of him with people, Ms. Stuart. We have other proof. We'd been letting him run loose because he could lead us to bigger fish. He had quite a game going, but he was still just the go-between. Last night he was killed by one of his customers. We're not sure why."

Numbly she let his words flow over her. Yussuf's killer was a terrorist named Ballieu. He was after some film. The deal had been scheduled to take place at Yussuf's next booking.

Serafin had told her Yussuf planned to retire after his next booking. What she was hearing must be true. She sat erect to keep her head from sliding into her hands in grief.

Now Oliver Lemming was asking her to work with them. To pose as the heir to Yussuf's empire. They'd provide her with names, make her story convincing, be on hand to protect her. They wanted her to substitute a flawed piece of film for the good one, through sleight of hand.

"You could help us put away a lot of people who'd otherwise be out hijacking planes and planting bombs," he said soberly. "You could save a lot of lives."

Did they know?

Channing's fingers slid across the desk toward the photograph, the one possession that made this room hers now. Tony. Still in his surgeon's clothes. His arm around her on a day they had laughed together.

She owed this to him, for the things he had believed in.

She owed it to cancel out what Yussuf had done.

But was she good enough?

The man by the window was watching her hand on the photograph frame. His expression was too alert. He was seeing too much. Channing turned the picture facedown and took her hand away.

"You think I can do it because Ballieu saw me with Yussuf. I'd play Yussuf's next engagement so it looks like I'm taking over his cover, his network, everything."

She repeated it back like a parrot. It wasn't fear that kept her from a decision, only uncertainty that she could bring it off. Yes, she could do coin tricks, card tricks . . . but a full twenty-minute act coming after some vocalist or stand-up comic? And could she look into the eyes of a man who had done what Ballieu had done and pretend to play games with him?

"We've got forty-eight hours to get into position—one plan or another," said Oliver, rising. "We've got to have your answer tomorrow. Bill will check with you."

From his spot by the window Ellery spoke through his teeth.

"It's dangerous. Do you understand that?"

She nodded mutely. Her head was reeling with the truth about Yussuf. She wished they'd leave. Bill Ellery shrugged and moved past her desk.

"I'll be in the middle of Venice Beach tomorrow at four," he said. "At one of the jewelry stands."

And then they were gone. Channing drew a deep breath, leaned back in her chair, and tried to think. She wished now she hadn't made herself responsible for Serafin, but once she started something, she didn't back down. Walking to the window where Bill Ellery had stood, she threw it open. It was going to be hot today, and Rundell was going to scream about wasting the air-conditioning, but a little fresh air always helped her brain.

Ballieu, as he drove past the house for a second time, saw a window open. It hadn't been, on their first pass at seven this morning. He wondered if this Khadija they had sent with the money, this female with insolent eyes who was supposed to help him, had been so observant. Ballieu had chosen to drive expressly so she could notice such things. Immediately she had resented it. She had sneered that today their organization believed in equality. She was one of the young ones, fat on her own importance. Ballieu was not pleased. He would have to teach her some lessons.

"An easy entry." The sneer was back in her voice. Her slitted eyes crawled up the house. "But unnecessary, with the meeting only two days away. We—"

"When there is any question, I do not take risks," Ballieu said coldly, interrupting. He had always worked alone before. He did not like explaining his actions. "This woman could spoil the meeting. The cassette the magician gave her could have names. Information about our organization. Anything. She could make demands on us, as he did."

The cause of people's liberation would not be slowed by blackmailers. Let sniveling governments afraid to pull a trigger play that kind of game, he thought.

Khadija shrugged, her boredom evident. Her black hair was braided against her neck. She wore a tight jersey, tight slacks. Though she couldn't be more than twenty-two, years of conditioning showed in the curves of her body.

"You're in charge," she said, but a challenge showed in her eyes. And they burned too brightly. She was overeager. So passionate in her zeal that she might make a misstep.

Ballieu noted all. He would have to watch her carefully.

For the moment he knew by her fervor and training that she was more than capable of the job he had assigned her.

"Find the cassette," he said. "Then get rid of the Stuart woman."

Four

Channing stood in the study facing the portrait of the man known to his audiences as the Great Sebastian. After all these years it still hurt, the last things he'd said to her here in this study. She knew he hadn't meant them. Yet sometimes she'd wondered herself, *was* she a Stuart? Knowing the skills she'd . . . been born with, maybe . . . had she turned her back on her birthright?

She toyed with the smooth old wand she'd picked up. Gramps's wand. What the men who'd just left wanted from her wouldn't be easy. Could she do it?

Behind her she heard the soft whisper of the door opening. She turned to see Serafin standing motionless just inside it.

"You're going to dump me, aren't you?" he said. "So you can help them."

Channing caught in a breath.

"You were listening!"

"It's okay." His voice was flat. "It doesn't matter."

Hard on the heels of her anger came a realization that he'd heard about Yussuf. If it had shocked her, how much harder had it hit him? Channing moved quickly, catching his shoulder and spinning him as he started to leave.

"Serafin. Listen to me. I have to help them. I've seen what people like the man they're after do. I don't mean to Yussuf, I mean to innocent people. To someone I cared for, who could have saved thousands of lives—"

She heard, suddenly, the vehemence of her own anger. As though it had lain hidden, like the water she often sought, it came rushing to the surface, tapped by the visit from the State Department men. Channel it. Capture it. Pipe it to where it served some purpose or it would be wasted.

Her voice softened. The boy before her had been betrayed by Yussuf. He wouldn't be betrayed by her. She wasn't going to vanish on him like some dove turned into a silk scarf.

"I'm not going to dump you, Serafin." She searched for the words that would make them both comfortable. "I figure we were sort of meant to be a team. You keep Rundell out of my hair and I'll teach you magic. Right now I need to practice. I'm not sure I can do what those men want me to do, and I've got to find out. What do you say?"

His face relaxed into the precursor of a smile. He looked almost as boyish as his twelve years. As she retreated toward the desk he nodded shy encouragement.

"Your grandpa's notebooks would probably tell you all kinds of things. Hints and stuff."

In the midst of scrabbling through the central desk drawer, Channing jerked to attention. How did he even know the notebooks existed? Or that she'd been hunting the key to the very drawer where they lay?

As though she'd spoken the questions aloud, he shrugged, his dark eyes on her.

"I can tell what people are thinking sometimes, that's all. Mr. Yussuf said I have a gift."

She let her breath out slowly. No. Growing up in this house, she certainly knew what was possible and what wasn't. She pointed the wand that was still in her hand to underscore her words.

"Nothing occurs that can't be explained by natural phenomena. No good magician claims they do. So no more of that. And no more eavesdropping. Understood?"

She tossed the wand to him, releasing the bright bouquet of flowers that popped free as he caught it, startled and delighted.

"Now," she said, "tell Rundell if he lets anyone else in to see me today, I'll fire him."

Not that Rundell would believe the threat, but it sounded good.

She'd look at her grandfather's notebooks; call a friend at the State Department to confirm that these two men who'd visited her were really employees, though they'd probably be listed as archivists or something; think about what she could put together for a twenty-minute act. Then she'd better find a piece of film to practice with.

It was like stepping into another world, one viewed through glass yet never experienced, as Channing immersed herself in hours of practice. Of course she'd put together little shows in her youth. She'd performed at hospitals with her grandfather, appeared in school talent extravaganzas, been booked at a nightclub or two while she was in college. Yet she'd never felt driven like this, never felt this compelling need to pull something from inside herself that went beyond skill.

It was that consuming force that had burned in her grandfather.

And her father? He'd died when she was five. She could hardly remember him. His car had gone off a bridge and he, a renowned escape artist, and her mother, an accomplished swimmer, had both drowned while she floated free.

Twenty years later, in Beirut, she had been a survivor once again. Inexplicably. Through some whim of fate. And she'd cursed deaf gods, asking, Why? Why was she spared? For what had been requested of her this morning? she wondered as she tried to knot two silks of different color together, producing a larger, checkered one. Her skill and interest lay in close-up magic, but she needed flashy tricks for stage work, some she hadn't tried in years.

"You have to eat!" protested Rundell, marching in on her at two that afternoon.

"All right. Outside," she said. She had polished several tricks with silks now.

In the garden behind the house she walked, a sandwich in one hand, one of her grandfather's notebooks in the other.

"This is what it's like?" asked Serafin in bewilderment.

"This is what it's like. All day. Every day. If you want to do it."

He followed her back to the study, and she showed him the simplest palm while she practiced her coins. He still was trying it, by lamplight, when he fell asleep.

"Just what are you going to do with him?" hissed Rundell as they walked the boy to bed.

Channing grinned.

"I've got friends in high places, Rundell. I expect everything to be ironed out."

"I expect to see you in jail!" he said crisply. "And I don't understand this practicing for a magic show. Aren't you gone enough?"

"Charity gig," said Channing. "I want you to check the thread in that gold jacket Gramps had made for me aeons ago. I'll fit it tomorrow."

Rundell, at some point before she'd been old enough to remember, had been Gramps's assistant. He understood the fitting and rigging of jackets. He sniffed and went off muttering to himself.

As soon as she turned back toward the study, her pretense of levity faded. Why couldn't Gramps, at some point in his life, have made just a few notes about the palming of film?

She knew why, of course. Film had no eye appeal. It wasn't shiny like coins or large and familiar like cards. No magician would think of using it.

But if she agreed to what those men from the State Department wanted, she'd have to use it. Lying back on the couch in the study, she brought out the piece of 35mm negative she'd been working with on and off all afternoon. She tried to maneuver it with fingers that worked coins, cards—even Yussuf's gun last night—with skill.

The negative stuck to her flesh. She wiped her fingers and tried again. Static. That was one problem. Another was the very thinness of the film itself. Another was the way it curved.

After half an hour she could see hardly any improvement in the adroitness of her motions. Sometimes she could get the film to vanish, but sometimes she fumbled it. Any trick, to be successful, had to be successful one hundred percent of the time. In this case the figure ought to be one hundred and fifty percent.

Bone-weary, she looked up at framed posters proclaiming her ancestors and their skills: "The Amazing Dr. Stuart," her great-grandfather, in his flowing white beard and garb of the 1890s; "The Great Sebastian, illusion and sleight of hand," her grandfather; "Charles Stuart, escape artist extraordinaire," her father. Three generations waiting on her.

For the first time in a long time she yearned for the moral support of Tony's arms around her. She burned with loneliness, the unleashed emotions angering her. She'd stretched herself so tightly since then, determined not to let her life become entwined with anyone else's, determined not to know loss again. And now those men who'd come this morning had made her think of things, had made all the old pain come flooding back.

Too discouraged to move, she reached up and snapped off the single light that glowed above her. If she napped for a few hours, she could try again.

She was deep in slumber, lost in a land of restless and vaguely unpleasant dreams, when she began to realize that something moving on the fringes of them wasn't a dream. She tried to fight her way free, back to a memory of where she was and to wakefulness. Even as her surroundings came into focus, Channing became aware of a presence in the room. A shape. A figure. There at the desk.

It was too tall for Serafin, the set of the shoulders wrong for Rundell, who wouldn't be prowling, anyway. And she didn't have her *kunjar.* Always, when she was far from civilization, she slept with it under her mattress.

The figure was hunting for something, opening desk drawers. Channing's fingers searched the floor beside her for a weapon. All they found was a heavy jade bookend that Serafin must have moved from the lower shelf of a table at the head of the couch. Its uneven shape made the chance of good aim unlikely. She grasped it, anyway, planning.

"Hunting for something?" she asked in a clear voice.

The figure snapped upright. Channing let fly the bookend. The figure dodged. As Channing sprang, groping futilely for the light, the intruder dove through the open window.

Yelling to summon Rundell, Channing crossed the room. She'd barely had time to reach the window when the houseman came huffing in with a flashlight he brandished like a club. In his other hand was a can of Mace.

"Someone was in here," Channing said grimly.

That someone wasn't lying on the ground below, either. He'd survived the two-story drop. He'd been agile and skilled.

"I'll call the police," said Rundell.

"Let's see what's missing first."

A gnawing in her stomach told her there might be some connection between the intruder and the visitors she'd had that morning. If there was, she'd better not contact the police. At least not until she could discuss it with Bill Ellery, and that wouldn't be until four that afternoon.

The house had been gone through thoroughly: drawers opened; pictures moved back in hopes of finding a safe; books, records, and tapes pulled off the shelves that held them. Her own bedroom was a particular disaster. Whoever had done the ransacking must have been a professional not to have roused anyone. Whole bureau drawers had been upended. But nothing was missing.

"Perhaps someone thinks you bring back drugs from those trips of yours," Rundell suggested.

Channing shot him a look. He could be a shrewd old prune at times. And a good one—he'd gone to check on Serafin as soon as they'd left the study. She supposed what he was suggesting was possible. There were occasional break-ins in this neighborhood, just as there were in so many other areas these days.

"Not that things look that much worse than they usually do when you get back," said Rundell. He grunted, retrieving a pair of shoes and the black magician's dress she'd discarded on the back of a chair two nights ago. Last year he'd served notice that he didn't intend to pick up her clothes anymore, but now he carried them methodically to the closet. "You know, I won't always be here to pick up after you, madam. Shall I fix you a nightcap?"

Channing caught the concern in his sideways glance as he smoothed her dress on its hanger.

"Make one for both of us," she said. "And don't

worry, I'll call the police tomorrow. I know a detective."

The lie didn't seem to persuade Rundell, so she pecked his cheek. That always unhinged him.

Bill Ellery shoved aside the file he'd picked up from the Federal Building that morning. He paced his hotel room wishing he knew less than he now did about Channing Stuart. The reports filtered in through the U.N., State Department, and FBI made a bright mosaic of a woman such as he'd never met before. Her skills at magic would have been enough. Or the crazy job. But now he knew that she'd once pulled a knife and driven off two men attacking a girl in an alley; that she'd reported an engineer she suspected of passing things to the Soviets (she'd been right); that her fiancé had been blown apart in a restaurant in Beirut.

He figured it was the fiancé that was motivating her to do this. Dumb, her taking this risk because of something in the past. But he figured he didn't have any right to mention that. It was personal. Like when he'd turned his back on the bar exam he'd never wanted to take in the first place, kissed a law degree and his share in the family fortune good-bye, and found himself in this job.

Part of the job was following orders. If Oliver and the powers-that-be thought using Channing Stuart was the best way to get that film back, then he'd give the sort of backup he was supposed to. All the same, he didn't like feeling responsible for her. She was inexperienced, no matter how gritty, no matter how sure of herself she looked when she stood with her hands on her hips. He'd hate to see blood leaking out on that creamy, freckled skin.

With a frown he realized he was growing interested in Channing Stuart. No time for that, Ellery. No sense risking it, either.

He picked up a light jacket that would hold the items he had to carry and set out to meet her. Maybe she'd change her mind. After all, she'd taken in that kid and might be getting all wrapped up in mothering him.

At four o'clock the breeze off the ocean was cool. He was glad for the jacket. As he made his way toward the boardwalk he was jostled by the usual assortment of girls in beachwear, kids on skateboards, teens with boom boxes. He grinned to himself. While privacy had been his first consideration in picking this site, he'd also thought the well-heeled lady Ph.D. might feel a little off-balance here. If they did work together, he wanted it clear from the start who was in charge.

A pair of kids on roller skates zoomed toward him, splitting to pass. He was in an area lined with open-air stalls selling handbags, sunglasses, tie-dyed dresses and other assorted merchandise. Directly ahead, a booth displayed chunky jewelry made of seashells and hammered metal.

There was no one at the jewelry stand but a young couple holding hands and a woman in an oversize beach hat, her back toward him. She had great legs. And no freckles.

"Free drink at the Sand Flea?"

A seedy youth pushed a coupon at him as Ellery

debated whether to wait there or press on toward another jewelry stand.

"No th—"

The rest of the word dangled off his tongue into midair. The body beneath the beach hat had turned. It was Channing Stuart, in as brief an orange bikini as he'd ever seen. The white shirt she wore over it, which from the back suggested sedateness, in front framed curves that were lithe and youthful. She grinned at him, and the laughter in her eyes told him he must be gaping at her exactly as other men had at finding her so unmistakably female.

That grin set her apart, somehow. It wasn't a smile drawn carefully to placate or attract. It was easy, natural, and went all the way to her eyes. It expressed nothing more than amusement—and maybe a warning of sparks if she got crossed.

She took the first step, and Ellery moved, meeting her halfway. She wasn't out of her element here at all, he realized irritably.

"I'm going to do it," she said, falling into step beside him. She kept her voice low. The quick humor on her face didn't hide its determination.

Ellery felt an unexpected frustration.

"Do you know what you're getting into?"

"I think so. Look."

Reaching into the pocket of her voluminous shirt, she produced a piece of 35mm negative, displayed it to him, and arched an eyebrow. Her hand turned lazily in a half circle, palm up, and the film was gone.

It was unsettling how she could do that. Some

kind of trick, of course. Ellery freed himself from the brief, trancelike state the act had created in him and reached inside his jacket.

"Why don't you try this?"

The blank film he extended to her was three inches by five, the same size as the one to be recovered. He could see her dismay. It was bigger than her whole palm. Surely now she'd back down.

One quick glance at his face, and her own filled with resolve.

"Almost the size of a card. It'll be easier."

The kids on roller skates shot by again. He could feel his frustration mounting. He caught her arm, intending nothing more than to steer her and to keep their conversation confidential.

"Why? When you stand a very good chance of getting a hole in your neck like Yussuf did? Just tell me that."

She pushed his hand away.

"Because I'm going to do it! That's all. And I'll need another piece of film just like the one you brought."

They were passing a T-shirt stand. She stopped and unfolded a pink shirt, holding it up so they'd look like anyone else just here for an afternoon of fun.

"So where do I go? And when? I gather you're not thrilled about working with me. I can't help that. I'll do what you tell me, how you tell me, and if something goes wrong, I knew what I was getting into. It's not on your conscience. Okay? I've made financial provisions for Serafin."

Her control impressed him more than emotion

could have. Anyway, it was her decision to make. He took the pink shirt from her and tossed her a green one.

"You go to the Palacio Sol. Tomorrow."

"He was booked there?"

No names. She was good at this.

"Right. You're picking up his schedule, starting the next day. Management's expecting you. I'll be there the morning after you get in."

They began to walk again.

"And the man I'm to meet?"

Ballieu, she meant.

"Yussuf had two suites reserved for people beginning the day I arrive." He frowned. The suites were reserved for two nights. He didn't understand that part. Why wait around? "We'll be just north of the Mexican border," he said. "Easy run if Ballieu needs to make it. Have fun in the sun, but don't drink the water."

"I thought it was throat problems I was supposed to watch for," she said.

The tart humor, bouncing off his heavier effort, startled him. He relaxed a little.

"Here," he said, sliding a photograph out of the envelope that had held the film he'd given her. "Take a good look at Ballieu. Make sure you recognize him."

She took a long, thoughtful look and then nodded.

They stopped in front of the Venice Beach Athletic Club, an outdoor affair where a few men in sweatbands were working out inside a pen. Beyond, across a stretch of sand, surf crashed and children squealed happily, making what they were discussing seem all but unreal. Time to separate, he thought.

"Any questions?"

Removing her hat, she brushed back her hair. It smelled of the ocean. She'd been swimming. Ellery experienced a sharp and jolting vision of how it would feel to swim beside her, far from the crowds, far from shore, testing your limits.

Her eyes were on the distant waves.

"Someone broke in last night. Searched the house. Nothing taken. Do I tell the police?"

Again her calm impressed him.

"First time in your neighborhood?"

"No. There've been a few others."

He rubbed the back of his hand against his lower lip and thought aloud. "Coincidence, maybe. Nobody knows about your part in this but me and Oliver and possibly his boss. Unless someone already thinks you were mixed up with Yussuf," he added grimly.

He half intended it as bait, but she looked as perplexed as he was. Shrugging, he raised a hand in departure.

"See you at Fun City."

"Ellery."

He turned back sharply at her voice.

"I have a price for this."

He hadn't thought she was that kind. Her words disappointed him.

"Sure. You'll get a per diem."

"Not cash." Her hands were planted on her hips. "Serafin's an illegal. I want him naturalized. And made my ward. Or I don't leave tomorrow."

He was motionless, not sure whether he was feeling anger or the impulse to laugh. Also not sure anymore whether he could believe her earlier promise to do what he said, the way he said to do it. He bit his words off, filled with sarcasm.

"Anything else?"

He thought her lips twitched once.

"One thing. I expect your people to pick up the bill for my underwear."

He eyed her narrowly, trying to figure out what she was getting at and not giving her the satisfaction of asking. But her eyebrows raised. She knew he was stumped.

"Silk panties cause static, which I don't need handling film, Mr. Ellery. I'm damned if I'll wear cotton ones at my own expense!"

Five

At Christmastime, Channing always received a card from her local jeep dealership. They loved her. She changed models yearly, equipping them with high-priced extras. The one she drove through the hot, barren stretches of southernmost California was blue, and she was glad of its reliability. Compared with the traffic in Los Angeles, this stretch of highway winding toward the plush Palacio Sol was all but deserted.

Seeing a service station ahead, she decided to pull over. Her work in remote places had conditioned her to feel more comfortable when her gas gauge read almost full. Besides, she wanted a cool drink. As she pulled up next to the tanks and jumped down, she heard a muffled pounding from the back of the jeep where her luggage was stowed.

"Channing! Let me out!"

She stared. Every bone in her body went hard with anger, vexation, and sudden fear. Whipping out keys, she unlocked the large old trunk that held her stage props.

"Serafin! What the hell are you doing in there? You could have suffocated!"

He looked penitent, and despite his dusky skin, she could see he was flushed.

"It's got a good lock. I thought I'd be able to open—"

"If I hadn't heard you, you could have died in there. Understand? *Muerto!*" She was feeling progressively weak with the aftershock.

He hung his head, brushing rivulets of sweat from his neck.

"You said we were going to be like partners. Partners stick together." His eyes turned up, pleading. "I want to make sure you stay okay. You're going to this place because of that spy business, aren't you?"

"Not another *word* about that," she said between her teeth, and to the attendant who approached them, "Fill it."

Grabbing Serafin's shoulder, she began to march him toward the service station.

"Don't get sore," he said, and his expression undermined the toughness she knew she should muster. It told her better than words that he was afraid of being alone. He was afraid of losing her. Maybe he was even afraid her promises wouldn't be kept.

She shoved him toward the men's room.

"Go run water over your head. Lots of it."

When he returned, she handed him a cold canned soft drink.

"You going to send me back?" he asked, his voice subdued.

"No," she said. She'd thought it over. Having Rundell come down to get him would cause more commotion than she wanted right now, and maybe a child's need for security had to count for more than logic in this case. "But don't you ever, ever pull anything like this again. Do you hear me?"

He nodded meekly.

"I can help you set up your props and stuff. I didn't mash anything."

They walked back toward the jeep. Out on the highway a car pulled off and meandered slowly by to stop at a curio stand a few hundred yards away. Channing frowned. It was brown with a vinyl roof. A small Cadillac. She'd swear it had been behind her when she'd left Los Angeles. She'd liked the color.

"Think there's something wrong with that car?" asked the boy beside her.

She recoiled slightly, irritated that her face had betrayed her thoughts. Serafin read people quickly. It was unnerving.

"Not a thing," she said. But the prowler two nights ago, on top of what she was about to do, made her edgy. "If you want to try reading my mind," she said, climbing into the jeep again, "try guessing the lessons I'm assigning you for tomorrow. I helped tutor a free-lance photographer's son last year. I have a fair idea what a kid your age is supposed to be learning."

He gave her a somber, unruffled smile. She checked the license plate of the brown car as she passed it. Final digits: 321. Then they made their way through the hot afternoon toward Palacio Sol.

It was a high-priced resort carved out of the desert. Three pools. Tennis courts. Golf and horseback riding. Palm trees and irrigated flower beds made the grounds that housed it an oasis. There was an outdoor art exhibit, and music wafted from one of the numerous lounges. The nearest town was a wide spot ten miles away. Closer to the resort, a few dusty paths suggested an occasional private dwelling lost somewhere in the scrub beyond. Before they had even finished registering, an assistant manager came bounding out to welcome Channing.

"We're so pleased you could fill in for the gentleman who was booked here," he burbled, taking her hand. "A terrible tragedy."

More than you'll ever know, thought Channing. For whatever Yussuf had become, he had been good once.

"I didn't realize you had an assistant," the manager said. His name was Wilbur. He was bald on top but preening for her all the same. With a look of concern at Serafin, he leaned closer to her. "Is he old enough to be in the club?"

"I'm a midget," said Serafin, deadpan.

"Oh." Wilbur's face turned red.

Channing closed her eyes to hide their rolling.

"Well. We've put you in one of our bungalows. Gives our entertainers a little more privacy, we've found." He gestured gallantly after her luggage.

"I'll be along in a minute," said Channing. "I forgot something in the car."

Wilbur wasn't her type, and she wanted to study the layout of this sprawling complex. As she turned, a man on one of the lobby couches cracked open a newspaper. Paranoia, noticing that, she told herself angrily. There was no reason she should think he'd been watching her. Maybe her nerves weren't steady enough for this job.

Outside, just to reassure herself that she was

growing overimaginative, she scanned the parking lot. There it was, at the opposite end from her jeep, a small brown Cadillac.

Drawing a slow breath, she started to walk. Maybe it was Bill Ellery. Maybe he'd come early. She began to move casually toward the car, picking out details beyond. A shrub-screened path cut away toward what, by the sound of it, was one of the pools. She kept her eyes down, prepared to sweep across the license plate without slackening her steps. The last three digits were 321. Her thoughts raced in the disciplined confines she imposed on them. She moved toward the pool, saw someone appear from the sheltered path, looked up, and fought for breath.

The man facing her had piercing blue eyes. Straight blond hair. Aristocratic features except for rather thick earlobes. His face wore a studied pleasantness that might hide any emotion. It was Henri Ballieu.

He was looking directly at her, as though his eyes were taking a photograph. Channing felt the sudden and chilling realization that she was all on her own. Bill Ellery didn't arrive till tomorrow. She had no way of contacting him, or Oliver Lemming.

"Lovely afternoon," she said, summoning a lazy smile.

Prepare the ground for later, when she made contact, she decided.

A fraction of a second passed, and then Ballieu moved aside. Her nerves tingled as she entered the winding path without looking back, knowing he was behind her. Her ears strained, and for the first time, on a gut level, she understood what Bill Ellery had tried to tell her about this man: He was a killer. As likely to strike as she was to brush her teeth. And probably noiseless.

What was he doing here? He wasn't due till tomorrow.

By the time she emerged into the noise and hot concrete of poolside, her palms felt cold.

She found her way through the pool complex and past tennis courts down to the bungalows, locating hers by the number on the key Wilbur had handed her. Serafin, ensconced in the smaller of their unit's two bedrooms, was watching TV.

"No going out without me," she said, and made her face a blank so he couldn't see her worry. She didn't like this, being here on her own with Ballieu. Should she start the plan into motion? Prudence told her not to, without a backup. Besides, she hadn't been given the names of Yussuf's contacts that were supposed to establish her authenticity.

Closing the door to her room, she showered and changed. Then, removing the large piece of film from her purse, she started to practice. The cotton underpants helped. Or she was getting better. Maybe both. But her movements weren't as deft as she wanted. It had taken fifty hours of practice, at least, to perfect that trick with the coins she'd learned for Yussuf. She didn't have a hundred hours for this one. Grimly she repeated her movements over and over, the part that would make one piece of film vanish, the part that would make another piece take its place.

Outside, the sky grew dark. Stars pricked their

way into being. From the other side of the door Serafin's voice, apologetic, broke into her concentration.

"Channing? Should we get some supper?"

She glanced at the clock.

"Oh, Serafin! I'm sorry."

She opened the door.

"Just let me hang up a few things."

Her everyday clothes could wait, but her carefully rigged jackets and her black dress ought to go on hangers. She hung the black dress first, smoothing its seams and straightening its pockets. Her fingers hit something and she stopped, remembering, as she drew out a cassette tape.

"Instructions for a trick of Yussuf's," she said to Serafin's look of curiosity. "He gave it to me." She turned it in her hand. "I'd forgotten . . . and I don't think I feel like hearing it just now. Maybe never." She stuffed it down into the side lining of her suitcase. "Come on. I'm starved."

Still seething from Ballieu's tongue-lashing—and from her own failure—Khadija watched the woman and the boy who seemed to be with her leave their bungalow.

Now.

She had to find the tape or Ballieu would report her.

Bastard, she thought. He could have searched that house himself. Had he sent her to prove his own power, or was there something wrong with him? She'd seen him squeezing his belly.

Reluctantly she acknowledged that Ballieu's caution now seemed justified. The woman had come here. She knew something. She was a threat.

Khadija began to move through the darkness, a shadow in black slacks and high-necked black jersey. She was eager to even scores with this woman who had startled her two nights ago, who had come awake and thrown something so unexpectedly and made Khadija fail in her mission. Almost never had she been thwarted in something she set out to do for their cause—never by another woman.

She would not fail this time. American meddling had deprived her of a homeland. American money had bought the planes and weapons that had killed her mother and little sister. Americans were wolves who fed on the weak. Whether she found the tape or not, killing the Stuart woman would be a triumph for Khadija's people.

Glancing around to make sure she was unobserved, she unscrewed the light on the porch of the bungalow and in only a matter of seconds sprang the lock on the door. The thin black gloves she wore insured there would be no prints. Khadija felt increasing confidence. She was good at locks. Good at rearranging electrical systems. She would show the old bastard Ballieu how good she was. Then perhaps she would mock him with what she knew.

With penlight in hand she began a methodical search of the bungalow. She found what she was after so quickly, she was almost suspicious. Then she decided that was just like a rich American woman, hiding a valuable tape in the side of a suitcase. It proved how stupid and weak such women were.

Khadija stuffed the tape into her pocket, eyes slitted with pleasure. The easy part was all that remained. She removed the electrical switch plate inside the bungalow door. She made a small rearrangement in the electrical wiring. Coming in across the darkened porch, the first thing anyone was likely to do was reach for the light switch. It would look like an accident.

Stepping cautiously, Khadija carried the ice bucket from the dresser into the bathroom, filled it with water, and, when she was safely on the other side, door open behind her, upended it to leave a puddle where the Stuart woman would step. She gave the bucket a toss. It landed agreeably near the wetness, as though it had tipped over, the culprit in all this.

Allowing herself a brief, sullen smile of satisfaction, Khadija closed the door.

"Aw, Channing, can't I just play a couple more games?"

Channing sighed, glad to find that Serafin was a normal twelve-year-old, at least when it came to addiction to video games. They'd found the arcade when they went exploring the main lodge complex after dinner.

Now, at the edge of one of the terraces, she considered. He'd be safe in the arcade, and she had her *kunjar* around her waist. On the way to dinner one of the guests had complimented her on her belt.

"All right," she said, shelling out a couple of dollars. "Stay there, though. I'll come and find you."

Relieved to leave the party-time noise of the

lodge behind her, she made her way down a walk to the twisting path that led to the bungalows. Of all the resort's accommodations, these were the most private, probably designed for honeymooners, Channing thought. Each sat well back from the path and apart from its neighbors. As she reached the point where she'd leave the main path to walk toward her door, Channing stopped.

The light was out. It shouldn't worry her, yet she was starting to have the feeling of too many coincidences. The break-in, the brown car that had been behind her all the way from L.A., and Ballieu here . . .

"I help you, lady?"

A Mexican maintenance man scrambled up from his knees. He'd been fixing a sprinkler, she saw now. She hadn't noticed him there.

"No . . . no, it's all right, thanks."

But he'd seen the direction in which she was looking.

"That your cabin? With light out? You twist ankle? I go put on light inside so you can see some."

He brandished keys.

"No, don't bother—"

She started after him as he hurried to help. In the darkness she stumbled and dropped her purse, which spilled its contents.

"Damn!"

Probably she was just imagining things. She paused to sweep items back toward the mouth of her purse. Surely they'd made enough noise to scare off anyone waiting inside, hadn't they?

"I come right back with new bulb for porch," the

maintenance man called cheerfully over his shoulder.

He unlocked her door as he spoke and reached inside.

The darkened doorway seemed to explode in sparks, gold against black, a thin deadly fountain. Channing heard a terrible crackling, high-voltage buzz. She stumbled to her feet as his body fell.

Halfway there, her tightly strung nerves picked up a sound behind her. She whirled.

"Channing?"

The voice, her racing brain told her, belonged to Bill Ellery. He was coming toward her.

"How's everything going?"

The words sounded closer but she could just make out his shape against the backlit path. Her tongue froze.

He wasn't supposed to arrive till tomorrow! What was he doing here? She was suspicious of him. She was suspicious of Ballieu. She pitched her voice to reach anyone near, anyone in the neighboring bungalows.

"Help me!" she called. "Someone please help me! A man's been electrocuted!"

Six

Members of the resort's executive staff darted down the path to the bungalows like bees from a hive. Their hushed and frantic buzzing had nothing to do with the loss of a man's life, everything to do with business.

"Is the body covered?"

"Jesus! Let's hope they don't use a siren and spook the guests!"

"If the press shows up, you handle them!"

They jostled Channing as Bill Ellery began to steer her away from the area. His mouth was set. His grip on her elbow was half protective, half warning. Behind them, the entrance to her bungalow was being roped off. What few guests happened along were being rerouted with some story about a faulty transformer. Only minutes had passed.

"I thought you weren't arriving till morning." Channing fought to control her voice.

"I got restless."

Ellery pulled her out of the way as two more hotel officials came huffing toward the site of the tragedy.

"Are you okay, dear?" one of them asked, pausing to turn.

"Of course she's not all right!" snapped Ellery. "She's just seen a man electrocuted!"

He shoved her into a corridor of the lodge that

was mercifully empty. Channing felt glad for the bruising hold he had on her, even for his anger. Was it weak to feel shaken? This was the second time in four days she'd seen someone die.

"No one's supposed to know why I'm here, except you and Oliver." She kept her voice just above a whisper, the shaken feeling giving way to rage at last. All she'd felt, all her suspicions of these last few minutes, began to spew free. "That man was innocent—he died in something set up for me. And don't tell me you believe what happened was an accident! I never touched that ice bucket—never put anything in it to spill. For another thing, Ballieu's already here. I've seen him. How else can you explain what happened?"

Something crossed the surface of Bill Ellery's eyes. His tight lips parted as though to challenge her. Instead he shoved her, no more gently, through another door.

They were in one of Palacio Sol's many lounges, this one vest-pocket-sized and nearly deserted. Bill Ellery stopped at the bar and spoke to the bartender.

"Two double ryes."

Channing saw he meant well, but his blunt assumption that she'd drink whatever was offered annoyed her.

"Make one of those dry sherry," she said.

She heard his breath fume out as he let go of her elbow. His eyes swept down her once, as though he'd like to make her vanish.

Abruptly he turned aside as the bartender brought their drinks and moved on toward the opposite end of the bar to polish glasses. She could almost see the man next to her reining his temper.

"Okay," he said, his voice as low as hers had been and with an edge of hardness she hadn't heard before. "It probably wasn't an accident. Want out?"

His directness caught her off-guard. The admission crimped her nerves into tight, chilly bundles. Confronted with the chance to turn her back, to retreat into safety, she let her breath out slowly.

"No. I don't."

He paused with his glass to his lips, surveying her above the rim.

"Because of the doc who got blown up in Beirut?"

Channing's fingers contracted around the stem of her sherry glass. Indignant surprise made her suddenly hate the people who'd recruited her. That was her life, her private pain.

"How much do you *know* about me?"

He drank gingerly, eyes lowering now.

"Same thing I'd want to know about anyone I had an assignment with. Everything possible."

Deliberately, without answering, Channing downed her sherry. She held its bitter richness on her tongue, along with words she'd like to utter. Maybe she'd relinquished her right to privacy, her right to be a private citizen, when she'd taken this job.

"Look, your personal life's none of my business," said Ellery tersely. "I shouldn't have brought it up."

She shrugged. He was the one with experience. She had to trust that and swallow feelings if they were going to work together. Her life could depend on it. She'd had a moment of doubt when she'd seen him back on the path, unexpected and conveniently near the electrocution. Now his very hardness was making her trust him. Something had already gone wrong in this setup, but she didn't think he knew why, any more than she did.

He was studying her, but before he could speak, a young female employee with a china doll's face bustled in.

"*There* you are, Ms. Stuart! Mr. Jurgens said to tell you we're going to take extra special care of you for the rest of your stay. We've moved you to one of our best suites. The front desk has the key. Oh—and your bar tab's going to be on us."

She smiled brightly.

The business-as-usual attitude disgusted Channing.

"Jesus! Afraid of a lawsuit," muttered Ellery.

The similarity of his reaction made Channing draw herself in tightly, wary of having too much in common with him.

Serafin, she remembered suddenly. She'd told him to wait in the arcade, and that had been much too long ago. Now, as if summoned by her thought waves, his dark head appeared in the door.

Channing set her glass down, making visual contact with the boy over Ellery's shoulder.

"Wait a minute," said Ellery as he realized she was about to depart. "We've got things to discuss. What happened out there means something's wrong—you're at more risk than we'd counted on—"

He turned just as Serafin ducked out of sight.

Channing shook her head, unable to believe Ellery would pursue this tonight. Or that it hadn't occurred to him she might already have reached the same conclusions.

"I've had it for one day, Ellery," she said wearily. "If you want to talk, see me at breakfast!"

In the lodge's main lounge Henri Ballieu leaned easily against a crowded circular bar, awaiting confirmation that the woman working with him had been successful. At its far end the room where he waited had scores of tables and a fair-sized stage on which the second show of the evening was now under way. The glass in Ballieu's hand held the establishment's most expensive brand of Scotch, and from his vantage point he could see through an archway to a hall that led to hotel offices. He recognized the burst of activity when it came. Hotel officials scuttled down the hall in one direction, then scuttled back in greater number. They conferred in undertones. Setting down his glass, Ballieu strolled out to find if the girl Khadija had accomplished her task.

By the time he had strolled to the men's room and back, he had overheard enough snatches of conversation to realize something had gone wrong. A resort employee was dead, not the Stuart woman.

The scuttling officials were calling it an accident. Their main concern was keeping the incident from their guests. He was safe for the moment at least, he thought angrily, resuming his place at the bar and ordering another drink, which he did not touch. Still, he was annoyed. This was what came of depending on someone else. The group in Paris had forced an assistant on him. Now she had failed where he would not have. The important question, he thought, resisting an impulse to rub at his chin and betray inner tension, was whether she'd recovered the tape.

He wouldn't make contact tonight. She had bungled and she might be under surveillance. Something in her inexperience might have aroused suspicion. He'd have to wait until morning—and plan.

Of course, he could pull out. A car with the key hidden under its license plate had been left along the road for him—just as one had been left on a street in Los Angeles. In case he'd arrived and sensed problems, there'd been that provision for escape. At dawn, if he hadn't taken the car, it would be reclaimed. Once past that time, there would be no further opportunity to scrap this assignment. He'd be committed to seeing things through, sending only a brief message to alert those waiting on the other end when and where to pick him up.

Ballieu didn't intend to pull out. That would be defeat. He would begin now to weave a net of safety for himself.

His eyes scanned the crowd.

It took ten minutes to select an appropriate woman: plump, pleasant-looking. In a dress that was slightly too girlish for her. And alone. It took an equal amount of time to establish visual contact with her several times.

Finally, as she ventured a hopeful yet circumspect peek, Ballieu moved in. He smiled first, with a little nod, then stirred from his place at the circular bar and walked toward her.

"It's a terrible thing to watch a show like this alone," he murmured, stopping at her table. "May I join you, or are you waiting for a jealous lover?"

She laughed with embarrassed delight at the compliment of his latter words—as he'd known she would.

"I'm not waiting for anyone," she said. She was blond, artificially so, and older than Ballieu himself. Several good-sized diamonds glinted on her hands as she made a nervous gesture to the chair facing hers.

"Harry Cardwell." Ballieu reached his own hand across the table to take hers in introduction. He let his fingers linger. She looked pleasantly flustered.

"Mildred Farrow," she whispered over the vocal duet that was starting on stage.

"You're not really here alone?" asked Ballieu with pretended disbelief.

"Well . . . yes . . ."

She seemed a bit hesitant. Ballieu sat back, taking care not to crowd her. He must go easily, he saw now. She'd be put off by too much charm.

"May I offer something to drink? You're so kind, sharing your table."

He'd let himself sound vaguely European. It appealed to women. Her round face relaxed.

There was a pampered gullibility about Mildred Farrow that reminded Ballieu of his aunt, who had suffered him and his mother to occupy a spot in her household as poor relations, obligated for the crumbs they received. His aunt had been a dull woman, never questioning the luck that had left her comfortable and others poor, just accepting it as her due. Looking down on those who were less fortunate. Judging. Giving orders.

Ballieu smiled. He spoke the rhetoric of the bourgeoisie now. It allowed him to fit in and better serve his cause. But he felt for the woman across from him the same contempt he'd felt for his aunt.

"I'm afraid I'm not very good at the bachelor life," Ballieu said, launching into easy fabrication of how his wife had died. He had realized long ago that women saw a widower as safer, somehow, than a bachelor.

Having a woman on the string was insurance. It was sometimes a source of useful information. It would also be, in this case, a way of diverting undue attention from occasional brief contact he might need to have with his female assistant.

"It's hard getting used to things without someone you've lived with," Mildred Farrow said, her defenses vanishing. "My husband's been dead three years. . . ."

Inwardly Ballieu celebrated his victory. Breaking the ice with a woman was always more useful than doing the same thing with a man. Women read more into it. They defined themselves in terms of men. Be nice to a woman and she construed it as interest. She would tell anyone who asked that you were nice. She would lie for you in a pinch.

Besides, on the rare occasions when it became necessary to take a ready-made hostage, people were always more protective of a woman.

Seven

By morning the resort looked to Ellery like the sort of place that would have attracted his parents and Reid: sprawling, equipped with all the upper-class amenities, and booked to capacity. A hell of a place to square off against someone like Ballieu. Which was exactly why Ballieu had picked it.

Savoring the last cool breeze the morning was likely to offer, Ellery stopped to study the walks leading into the main building from the pool and outdoor dining areas. It was seven A.M. He'd been roaming the halls and paths of the resort for almost two hours. In his mind he went over its layout, where every door led, the location of power panels, sprinklers, walls that were likely to stop bullets instead of letting them ricochet. Tension tugged at his insides.

Ballieu didn't play by the rules. Ballieu, in those rare, tight situations where he'd come close to being trapped, had taken hostages. Insuring the safety of Channing Stuart in a place like this was going to be a problem.

"Breakfast, sir?"

A waiter's voice made Ellery realize he'd paused too long on the outdoor dining terrace, measuring the walkways. He was irritated by his slip into visibility. To his way of thinking, it verged on carelessness.

"Orange juice to go," said Ellery. "Great place here."

They'd be burying Sam this afternoon, and he wouldn't be there. It felt wrong, missing that final good-bye, but Sam of all people would have understood. Better to prevent another death here if that's possible, huh, Sammy?

He signed for the juice and strolled, sipping it. He hoped Channing Stuart was still asleep. He hoped she wasn't given to panic. She'd seemed close to it last night.

Oliver had promised to pull another team from somewhere to send in, but so far Ellery hadn't seen any sign of familiar faces. If he had to keep a really tight watch on Channing Stuart, he hoped Ballieu would take him for nothing more than a red-blooded male on the make.

Eyes squinting slightly, he marked sections of walk against the range of the .38 hidden beneath his light jacket. The gun wasn't going to be much good once these walks and dining areas filled up with people.

That was the difference, he thought. His side had rules.

Henri Ballieu's side didn't.

Henri Ballieu had been seventeen when he discovered how easy it was to kill someone, and how much it accomplished. Rarely did he recall such moments from his past. When he did, it usually annoyed him. This morning's memory returned to him with pure satisfaction, dislodged, no doubt, by last night's encounter with the woman who resembled his aunt.

Shutting off his electric razor, Ballieu slapped after-shave onto his cheeks. It was still a bit too early to be out and about in a place like this without attracting notice. He slid a long, razorlike blade just inside the pack of cigarettes he would carry, and let the memory of his uncle's execution flow into him.

Ballieu's mother had been taken in, in disgrace, when the foreigner who'd made her pregnant had abandoned her. She'd sewn and cooked like one of the servants, and Ballieu, as soon as he was old enough to carry trays of lead type, had been sent to work in his uncle's print shop. Day after day he'd worked his muscles sore while his cousin of a similar age, who would own the shop someday, spent his afternoons drinking tea with girls and reading poetry. Seething at the inequity, Ballieu had become aware that there were individuals in the streets who spoke aloud of such injustices between the classes. Mostly they were university students, little better off than he was himself.

Gradually he had become a part of one of their groups. They had needed political pamphlets run. Ballieu had run them on his uncle's press. His uncle had fired him.

One of the students thought he could make plates for currency.

"Do it and I'll run them," Ballieu said.

He himself studied paper and ink that would give an authentic effect. They needed financing for a people's revolution. It would rob men like his uncle of their bloated status and carefully guarded wealth. It would put bread in the mouths of hungry children, dignity in the labor of workers.

When his uncle came in unexpectedly in the midst of their venture, Ballieu raised a gun and shot him. He had been a bit too close. The blood had splattered his arm.

Commended for his work, Ballieu had been spirited out of the country. A larger, more organized group than the students had taken him in. It meant nothing to him to see his mother again. The passion for equality was in his blood.

He was eager to please his new comrades, eager to rise in their ranks. He had killed a policeman in a public square, the act well planned and calmly executed. He had kidnapped a municipal official. He was not yet nineteen.

The following week he had been approached by a well-dressed man smoking strong cigarettes.

"Why are you wasting time on provincial officials?" he asked. "Come to Paris. We can give you better targets. We can bring whole governments to their knees."

That had been thirty years ago. In the decades between, Ballieu had never felt so acutely the cold deliberateness that filled his veins now. He had felt it raising the gun to shoot his uncle—a sense of fate. Now it was underlaid by years of experience.

Ballieu smoothed his collar.

It was eight in the morning. By now a few golfers and tennis players would be stirring, eager to have their games before the heat of the day. He would not attract notice. Picking up a small tape recorder, shifting his cigarette package so his finger rested on the blade inside it, he walked toward the elevator.

He would ride two floors down. He would see whether anyone was watching the hallway. If they weren't, he'd discover whether the female helping him had, in spite of last night's blunder, recovered the tape.

"Well?" he demanded as she opened her door to him.

Her mouth was defiant.

"How was I to know some stupid worker would go in first? How was I to prevent it?"

No apology, no nervousness at her failure, only her sullenness daring him to upbraid her. She wore bright shorts, looking the part of a girl on holiday. Her black hair was free on her shoulders.

"The cassette?" Ballieu asked coldly.

She turned her back on him and crossed the room.

The cassette was hidden under a false bottom she'd glued into a leather bag. She ripped it free with fingers Ballieu knew were strong enough to strangle a man. She was not completely without qualifications. He snapped the tape into place, and they sat warily on either side of the low table with the tape player between them, the female's resentment now dying down into curiosity.

At first, as the words coming off the machine began to sink in, Ballieu thought they must be a trick. Disbelief, followed by a fleeting sense of disgrace and then anger, crowded out other feelings inside him.

". . . and the king of hearts is upside down . . ."

The magician's voice mocked him.

Everything mocked him. The way things were starting. The pain that cut suddenly into his belly. The look on the girl's face.

Her head tipped back, and laughter issued from her throat.

"A magic trick! You made me risk my life for a magic trick, Ballieu."

His fist slammed down, stopping the machine.

"Of course it could be a code," the girl suggested, and laughed again, the sound a sneer.

She didn't believe it. She believed his whole concern had been unnecessary.

Ballieu felt mounting rage. Under other circumstances he would kill her. Would send her away, at least. He had seen her kind before. She was a young jackal, sniffing, waiting for his body to fall. In her eagerness to see him trip, she would be careless herself. She could not be depended upon.

He swore to himself. The most important, the last mission of his life, and he was stuck with a female whose neck he would like to break. She had accomplished nothing—minor assignments, no doubt, which had swelled her ego. Yet she sat there looking confident. And he was dying.

"Maybe the Stuart woman tricked us," he said, focusing all his thoughts on that possibility as he rose and started to pace. "Perhaps she's smart. She must realize you were hunting something there in her study. Perhaps she knows we're watching her. And we can't risk another accident. Not after you bungled last night."

The girl in the chair ignited, springing up to face him.

"I didn't bungle! The electrocution went perfectly."

"Except that she isn't dead." Ballieu let his sarcasm lash her.

"Then I'll kill her some other way!"

"And start an investigation?"

It was his turn to sneer as he pointed out her inexperience. Her eyes narrowed into slits.

"Are you afraid, Ballieu? I'm willing to die for our cause! And perhaps you should tell me what we are here for—what we're to accomplish. If you make another error in judgment and are taken prisoner, I will have responsibility to finish here!"

Ballieu's open hand flew out, the force of his slap knocking her to the floor. She fell against the bed. She would learn her place if nothing else, he thought with satisfaction.

"The most important assignment we've had in ten years, and they send me a hothead with more rhetoric than common sense!" he said bitterly. "You have no need to know anything. You are an errand girl. You were sent to deliver the money sewn in your coat—and whatever else I choose to tell you. Learn to keep your mouth shut."

She pulled herself to her knees, one finger going to her bleeding mouth, then stoically moving away. Her eyes, thought Ballieu, suddenly noticing them for the first time. Where had he seen eyes like hers?

"I was sent because some people think the great Henri Ballieu is getting too old for jobs like this!" She spit the words at him. "That you've grown more interested in your own glory than in democratic liberation." In spite of the blood, her lip gave a curl of defiance. "Some think your judgment's not as good as it used to be."

Ballieu felt himself go motionless. Nothing could make him fail in this mission—not her, not her barbs. He would not let vanity goad him into making a misstep.

Glancing at his watch, he began to shrug casually into his jacket.

"Too much has gone wrong," he said, abandoning the argument he knew she would like to pursue. "We have to speed things up. Give me twelve minutes. Then meet me at the magazine stand."

With his eyes daring her to move, he unwrapped a peppermint candy and dropped the cellophane onto the floor. The peppermint would soothe the pain in his stomach.

"Be stuffing your blouse in as you leave here," he added. "Someone may be watching me. Nothing will be made of our contact if they think you were whoring."

He turned his back, confident her eyes were burning with hate. At the door he paused to look indifferently over his shoulder.

"We're here to pick up a piece of film designed to make U.S. passports. Your group has been promised first use. You'll be a heroine, Khadija—if you learn to take orders."

This was the way to train the young and too impulsive, he thought, closing the door behind him. Alternate parts of fear and reward. It kept them loyal.

This time the elevator took him down to lobby level. As he stepped out Ballieu made note of the time again, surveyed his surroundings for any faces that might be following him, and moved toward a row of pay phones. The booth he chose had been predetermined. He had allowed himself a cushion of nearly ninety seconds. Pretending to peruse the booth's directory, he waited, picking up the phone beside him on its first ring.

"Do you want to buy oranges?" inquired a muffled voice at the other end.

"A boxcar," Ballieu answered. "I have cash."

Now that contact was established, he found himself relaxing slightly. Things were starting to go according to plan. His eyes raked the lobby again. Then he spoke quickly.

"I want the transaction today—this afternoon."

The man at the other end must know by now that Yussuf was dead.

"Impossible," said the voice on the phone. "We have a problem. The magician put the goods in a safe. There's a timing device on the lock. If we try to open it before the scheduled time, the thing will blow."

Ballieu willed himself not to tense. Tension dulled his reflexes. He'd been careful to learn all the whens and wheres of this contact and had strung the magician along even when he knew he was going to kill him. Now, suddenly, there were complications.

"And those men in the alley?" he asked calmly.

"State Department. They've got two here watching you. Don't worry. That part's under control."

Could he chance it, or were the odds growing too

high against him? Ballieu found himself weighing decisions. He had nothing to lose; the gain to his organization would be invaluable. The knowledge of increasing risk and the challenge posed to his skills warmed his blood like whiskey, making him forget the pain in his belly. No one, not even the seller, knew he was not here alone, so he had an edge in the female helping him. He'd never seen the seller, wouldn't know him by sight, but arrangements for visual contact, just like for this verbal one, had been worked out.

"Where is the safe?" he asked.

He made notes quickly, then tucked them inside a travel brochure as he hung up. His hand was reaching to open the door when he saw the Stuart woman and a boy who seemed to be with her get off the elevator.

He studied her from his glass sanctuary. Poised. Not arrogant like the little bitch he was stuck with but with a way of holding herself that made him almost hungry. His eyes roved over her body again. Poise in a woman with nerve enough to dabble in danger was far more potent than perfume or low-cut dresses. This one was dabbling, or she wouldn't be here. He wondered when she would make her move, and how he would kill her.

Khadija was strolling toward the magazine stand. At least she was punctual. Ballieu went out to meet her. He bowed extravagantly as he handed her the travel brochure. If anyone was watching, they would not attach any significance to so obvious a gesture.

"There's a timing device to dismantle," he murmured. "Prove you're as competent as your group claims."

As she walked away, Ballieu felt instinct biting at him. For a final time he wondered if he was making the right decision. The man who was selling the film, who had been on the other end of the phone just a minute ago, was an amateur.

And the danger with amateurs was that they could panic.

Eight

Channing leaned against a palm tree watching workmen install a new porch light at the bungalow where, except for a fluke, she would have died last night. If ever she'd had any second thoughts about the commitment that had brought her to Palacio Sol, the death of the maintenance man had removed them, she thought. He'd been a victim, like so many others. Ballieu and his kind didn't care who they killed to accomplish their ends. Maybe she'd needed to be reminded. She shifted, trying to loosen the anger from her body.

The day was barely beginning, and already the sleeves of her white voile shirt felt warm. But she'd be wearing sleeves her whole time here. For what she'd been asked to do she couldn't count on a schedule, nor could she work bare-armed.

"You ever see anybody die before?"

Serafin was at her elbow before she even heard him. She tried to pull herself free of the thoughts that were holding her.

"Yes."

She didn't want to explain about Tony, or the little girl who had died in her arms in that blood-drenched restaurant. The dimming images had grown fresh in her mind again, pushing her toward unfinished business.

Rousing herself, she looked at him with forced cheerfulness.

"Don't tell me you've finished that math already."

He was wearing swim trunks they'd bought in one of the lodge shops last night. He studied her for a moment. His bottomless eyes took on a glimmer of smugness he couldn't quite hide as he passed her a paper.

"All correct, huh?"

She'd thought the work would stump him, or at least make him vow never to run away again. Now she realized she'd met her match in Serafin. It tickled her, the first thing all morning to seem remotely funny. She raised her eyes and saw his twinkling, too, and fought a grin.

"I can see it was too easy," she observed, returning the sheet of resort stationery.

She'd given him two of them, one filled with mixed fractions, decimals, and long division, the other with an essay question. They'd give some idea where he belonged in school when they got back to L.A. Besides, she wasn't quite sure what to do with a child twenty-four hours a day.

After last night she was more than a little concerned for his safety too. Yet sending him home would be harder today than it would have been yesterday. He'd been on his own. He was street-smart. When he'd tried on the swim trunks, she'd noticed a scar on his thin ribs, and he'd told her he'd gotten shot "just a little bit" crossing the border. She'd have to trust that her decision to let him stay with her had been right. Emotional wounds could be more fatal than physical ones.

"All right. Do the writing assignment, and then you can swim," she said.

Then what would she do with him?

He skewed his face into a look that was supposed to be reassuring.

"You're worried about me, huh, Channing? But I've figured it all out. I'll hang around with Wilbur—that bald guy who works here?—whenever you want me to. I'll tell him I'm interested in learning hotel management."

Channing choked. "He'd never believe it."

"Sure he will. He believed it when I said I was a midget. There's Ellery. I'll split."

She turned and watched as the boy bolted up the steps toward the dining terrace. How had he known Ellery's name? She hadn't mentioned a thing about the business she was involved in. Ellery stopped, thunderstruck, as Serafin rushed by. As quickly as they'd spotted the boy, his eyes swung back to her, driving in like nails.

There was going to be a storm now, and Channing moved toward it with relish. She knew Bill Ellery was in charge. She knew he was going to blow sky-high over Serafin's presence. But she also knew she wouldn't back down.

Ellery saw, from the glint in her eyes as she came toward him, that there'd be no budging her.

He tried, anyway.

"What the hell is that kid doing here?" he asked as they met at the edge of the terrace.

She moved past him without breaking her stride.

"He's my assistant."

She brushed between white wrought-iron tables that were shaded by green-and-white umbrellas and pulled out a chair before he even thought about doing it for her.

"He stowed away," she said, tossing her hair back. "And he stays. I'm not about to throw him out right after I've taken him in."

Ellery sat down slowly. He couldn't decide what to make of her. She seemed too intelligent to have any illusion that the job they were here to do was some sort of game. She sounded too definite. She knew the risk she was taking—with herself and with the boy.

It wasn't a risk to the job she'd been sent to perform, he decided. It wasn't his business.

"Sleep okay?" he asked.

He'd already seen the answer in the fine lines under her eyes. She looked up, surprised at his show of concern.

"I slept," she said, hedging, and unfolded her napkin as a waiter poured coffee.

Ellery decided not to back off. He wanted to know how her mind worked. How she thought. That was half the secret to being a team.

He frowned, disturbed again by the knowledge that he was responsible for her safety.

"Why are you so determined to do this?" he asked. Her commitment to the things she undertook could be a handicap. It could make her blind. Yet it was a part of her nature that attracted him. "Because of the doctor or because of what Yussuf did?" he pressed.

She seemed to hesitate.

"Both. Neither, maybe." She shook her hair back again. "Maybe I'm just trying to prove to myself I'm a Stuart."

Her words were brisk, but she helped herself to a croissant, avoiding his eyes. Ellery was quiet, putting the pieces together.

"Your grandfather say you weren't? When you picked geology over magic?"

She flicked a look at him. It showed surprise, then reluctant honesty.

"Yes. What about you? Why'd you choose this kind of work?"

The swiftness of her counter-interrogation left him with a wooden tongue. He wasn't used to having the spotlight turned on him, or that tone suggesting that what he did was special.

"Someone needs to," he said. "Better someone like me than someone with a family like Sam."

Her clear gaze made him shift in his chair. He could see she'd picked up on how close he'd felt to Sammy.

"Your partner?" Her voice had a softness he hadn't noticed before. But another voice cut across hers, jerking him to his senses.

"Well, well, well! If it isn't the superstar!"

Ellery looked up, pleased as he recognized the cheerful needling, and felt a sudden surge of optimism. This assignment might go better than he'd thought. Max Hopkins was one of the most alert and quick-witted agents Ellery had ever worked with. He was also the worst clotheshorse. Ellery observed him with dry amusement. Max's lanky form was all in white. His curly black hair was carefully styled. He wore a bracelet and the same scent that good old Reid the Senator wore—fifteen hundred dollars a bottle. Max spun a chair around and straddled it, tweaking Ellery's collar.

"When you going to buy a shirt with some life to it, Billy?"

"Channing Stuart, Max Hopkins," said Ellery.

If there was going to be anything enjoyable in this assignment, it would be watching Max and Channing square off for a few rounds. Max liked the ladies and was already giving Channing a covert once-over. Ellery could see him revving up the charm.

"Max and I work for the same firm," Ellery added.

Channing got the message and smiled. Max seemed to have no inkling of her role. Ellery filed the fact away. Maybe Max and his partner, Walker, hadn't been told. He'd play it that way until he checked with Oliver.

"Saw you arriving yesterday," Max said, extending his hand to Channing and displaying dazzling teeth that Ellery knew damned well had been capped. "You and a kid."

"We're the magic act," Channing said.

Max's pale blue eyes looked perfectly innocent, but Ellery knew him well enough to know that Max was figuring he could score.

"Channing?" He kept his voice soft but firm. "Max and I have some business to talk over."

Her lips pursed. Her eyes crackled once as they

met his. She wanted to argue but didn't, keeping the promise she'd made about obeying.

"Oh, you're about to lose a button," she said, bending toward him as she stood up. Before Ellery could blink, she reached out lightly with both hands and gave a tug at the front of his shirt. "There. Now you won't lose it."

A breath of anger welled up from Ellery's throat. He saw the satisfaction in her look. What the hell was this? There hadn't been anything wrong with his buttons. She'd pulled one off deliberately. He'd have to go change.

"Maybe I'd better sew it back on for you," she said, picking it out of his hand where she'd dropped it. She blew on the button, pressed it in place, and Ellery looked down to see the front of his shirt completely restored.

Max was gaping. Channing Stuart turned without another word. Ellery just sat there, provoked and startled. His senses had somehow deceived him. He'd *seen* the button unattached. He'd felt it in his hand.

"Ni-i-ice number," Max breathed as he watched Channing's backside move toward the lodge. "How'd she do that?"

Ellery shrugged.

Abruptly Max changed the subject, crossing his arms on the back of his chair and leaning against them.

"Listen, Ellery. You got all the glory for that job in Atlanta. This one's mine."

"Yeah?" said Ellery. Max was one of the few people he'd ever met who was so sure of himself, he didn't shrink from making demands like that. It allowed the two of them to rib each other without mercy. "Can I help it that you wrecked that flashy car you were driving and I had to bail you out?"

He'd never decided if the rivalry between them was real or pretended.

Max shook his head in pretended sorrow. "You don't spare the gonads, do you? I'd only had that car two weeks. Anyway, you owed me one for saving your ass in Prague."

Max appropriated the half roll Channing had abandoned and chewed with enthusiasm. Ellery grimaced inwardly. When Max wasn't trying to dazzle someone, he had the manners of a chimpanzee.

"Where's Walker?" Ellery asked.

"Listening post. We're set up across from Ballieu's room. Guess he got here last night. I'm his bird dog this shift. He's over there behind that planter. Thoughtful of him to wear handmade shoes so I can make him by his feet."

Ellery realized Max was far more alert than his casual appearance suggested. He had been watching all the time. Max brought his keen gaze back to Ellery.

"Sorry to hear about Sam."

Ellery nodded at the condolences.

"Glad you're here," said Max. "Walker's not in peak form—hasn't been for a couple of weeks. They sending you a new partner, or do you go this one alone?"

"I'm waiting for word from Oliver."

"Christ, how do you stand it, Billy? The man's a martinet."

Max's kidding streak reappeared. His head nodded toward the door to the lodge, through which Channing had just disappeared.

"On second thought, I'd rather know how a sorry s.o.b. like you met a broad like that."

Ellery hesitated, then decided not to fight temptation.

"She got lost between the elevator and the lobby," he said, keeping his face as straight as a poker. "A real airhead if you ask me. Just the kind you go for, as I recall."

He stood up and slapped Max's shoulder. He owed Max this.

"Yeah?" said Max with interest. "Holy shit, Ellery! What do you want in a woman? Einstein?"

Channing lifted the straw hat shading her face and wiped irritably at the band of moisture beneath it as she walked toward the archery range. The note the front desk had handed her had been marvelously to the point: "Archery lesson, 11:30. Ellery."

Bill Ellery didn't waste words.

She felt annoyed with herself for having pulled that trick with the button on him, but she'd resented his unvoiced message that he didn't consider her an equal in this operation. In retrospect she knew she wasn't. And it was that truth which she really resented. She was effective with magic, but how effective would she be going up against Henri Ballieu? She wasn't sure, and Ellery wasn't, either.

Even though it would grow still hotter as afternoon set in, the sun already scorched the unshaded patch of grass that was the archery range. Of all the resort's activities, this seemed to be the most remote, which no doubt explained its selection. Putting her forearm up against the glare of the sun, Channing saw the usual round targets set up on easels. She was glad to be acting finally, instead of waiting. There were figures at two of the targets. The nearer of the figures was Oliver Lemming.

"Bill's not here yet?" she asked in greeting.

The white-haired man who'd recruited her hadn't been in evidence at the resort. Maybe he was staying somewhere else.

"He'll be waiting in your room when you get back," he said, sighting down an arrow. "As soon as you leave here, we want you to make contact with Ballieu."

With a thunk the arrow he'd released sank into a bull's-eye. It seemed to underscore the gravity of his words. It also impressed Channing with the older man's physical conditioning.

"We want to make you valuable enough that Ballieu won't hurt you," he said, looking at her for the first time. "Tell him Yussuf had set up a double cross but that you can stop it if you're there when the film changes hands. The story's your insurance policy."

"And the names I'm to drop? Of Yussuf's people?"

"Marinka in London and Colón at the Banco Central in Managua. Got it?"

"Got it."

He sent another arrow home, then handed her a bow and quiver that rested nearby. With them, Channing felt a flat, heavy envelope pass into her hands. The full weight of her responsibility beat into her along with the sun. She realized the envelope held the doctored film.

Vanishing the envelope, she slid her middle fingers into a leather guard.

"Bill told me about what happened last night," said Oliver.

"That's not all."

It had been years since Channing used a bow, and as her shoulders moved out and back, the man with her tapped the inside of her left arm to correct her form so the string would clear. She waited until she'd released and her arrow had hit the very bottom of the target before she continued.

"Someone's been through my things." They were both pretending to watch the target, but she caught the sharpening of his expression. "I had a tape Yussuf gave me the other night. He told me it was instructions for a magic trick. It's missing."

"You're sure that was all that was on it?"

"I didn't play it." Hearing the swiftness of his question, she felt more chagrined than ever by the admission.

"Tell Bill?"

"Max Hopkins showed up before I got a chance. I was told to run along like a good little girl."

Oliver seemed lost in thought. He motioned her to try another arrow. This time her aim was better. He nodded approval.

"We'll go from where we are," he said. "It's all we can do. We're getting barbecued out here. Why don't you head on back?"

* * *

Her hotel room gave few hints of what Channing Stuart was like in private. Ellery noted Adler's *Six Great Ideas* beside her bed, and half dollars stacked on the dresser as if she practiced magic tricks while brushing her hair.

He heard a key in the lock, tensed to react in case it wasn't her, then relaxed as he saw it was. She secured the door and then took pointed note of how he stood. One of his legs was hitched easily up across the corner of her dresser. He'd assumed the posture from habit. He'd always been a leaner.

"Learn anything else about me by going through my drawers?" she asked. She wasn't pleased.

Ellery grinned.

"Damn." She realized how her words had come out.

"Just that you were serious about switching to cotton," Ellery said.

He figured she was irritated at his invasion of her privacy, but her safety depended on his hearing every word of the phone call she was about to make. She tossed her hat on the bed. He found himself unusually conscious of her movements.

"Let's get it over with," she said crisply. "Serafin's downstairs, and I don't like leaving him alone for too long."

"It's not my fault you brought him, is it?"

Ellery heard his voice hardening. She looked cool and in control of herself in her white linen jacket, but her hands, as though moist, passed briefly over the legs of her slacks. She seemed to accept the reprimand. He wondered if beneath her hair-trigger reactions there might be a streak of common sense.

"Any last words of wisdom?" she asked.

"Just dangle enough bait to keep yourself safe."

They walked to the telephone.

She raised the receiver. He dialed. The unrehearsed coordination of their movements felt so natural and so perfectly timed that Ellery found himself holding his breath.

He tried not to notice her wetting her lips. He tried not to think how she could be safe, back in her comfortable home with her crotchety houseman. He wondered if she ever took the easy way out of anything. Then a voice snapped to life at the other end. It was Ballieu.

"Hello?"

Channing's lips shaped each word carefully. She looked across the mouthpiece, and Ellery realized she was watching his eyes to gauge the effectiveness of her performance.

"The deal with the film is in danger, Monsieur Ballieu," she said distinctly. "I can help you. Come watch the magic act."

She raised her eyebrows, sliding a finger across the base of the phone to break the connection before Ballieu could answer.

Bill Ellery nodded grim approval.

Step One was over. There was no turning back.

Nine

Ballieu strolled past the swimming pool, enjoying the heat of the sun on his body. It made him feel young again. He was shirtless and free.

A group of boys was splashing at the deep end of the pool, outdoing each other with leaps and belly-whoppers off the concrete. He could hear them taunting a younger boy who stood on the edge, afraid to dive.

Ballieu was fond of children. Especially the little ones. He flung out his arm, catching back the quaking boy of eight or thereabouts who, with tears in his eyes, was about to launch himself out.

"Hunch your shoulders forward and cut the water with your hands, eh?" whispered Ballieu. He pantomimed the hand position. "Then it won't hurt so much." He winked.

The boy stared at him in awe.

"Hey, thanks, mister!"

Folding up like a clam, the boy dove, came up, and waved triumphantly. Ballieu, feeling satisfied, walked casually to his appointment. He lowered himself onto one of the lounge chairs ringing the pool.

"Is the safe guarded?" he murmured to the woman who lay facedown in the chair next to his.

Khadija's slim, oiled body was as motionless as an

adder. Ballieu had just bought two drinks for a girl in a blue bikini. When he left here, it would be to make arrangements with a high-priced prostitute. With such attention to women, his occasional contacts with Khadija would not arouse undue notice.

"Only one, hired by the magician," she answered. "I left him in a storeroom. We'll be gone before the body starts to smell."

Under the pretext of applying sunscreen, Ballieu scanned the crowd and picked out a familiar face. He was sure now that he had identified two men watching him. One was black and looked out of condition; the other was flashy and white. They traded turns.

"The bomb is a new design, set to go off if even one of its wires is touched before the time elapses," the female beside him was reporting. "My group has seen only one, and it blew up the man who thought he could take it apart. But I believe a spray fixative might dull the contacts. I'll go back tonight—"

"No." Ballieu's command was soft but swift. "An attempt that fails would destroy the film."

He could see by the way her body stiffened that she disagreed with his decision. He was satisfied with her nerve, but she was too caught up in her zeal. Cleverness was their only chance now. And nerve. They were being watched. They were outnumbered, possibly. But they had the advantage of the Americans wanting to catch whoever was selling the film.

"We'll wait them out," he said aloud. "It takes more courage to walk with a bomb between your legs than to storm a camp with a rifle. We are walking with a bomb, and we will have our victory. Do you understand? Besides, we may have help. The Stuart woman called me—"

He broke off as Mildred Farrow, who last night in the lounge had shared a table with him, walked past, sending him a look and a hopeful flutter of her fingers.

"Bridge class at two," she called. "Are you going to come?"

"Of course," he called back cheerfully. "Would you like a partner?"

Beneath its layer of paint, Mildred Farrow's face broke into a smile. She had a bracelet around her ankle and painted toenails. Ballieu watched her buttocks, squeezed ridiculously into white pants, as she pattered off on high-heeled shoes.

"The Stuart woman called, and she wants a meeting," he said, resuming.

"It's a trick!"

"Perhaps."

He was noting the hate in Khadija's eyes as she watched the people around them. She had not been a wise choice to send amid Westerners. Her language was good, but she lacked sophistication. She didn't understand how much could be gained by playing a role.

She tried to sweeten her tone.

"Let's plan something more, Ballieu—something more than getting the film. Suppose something goes wrong? Suppose the call you got was a trap? Suppose we don't get the film—we could still accomplish something here that would make our trip worthwhile. Look around!"

Ballieu hesitated, coaxed by what she was saying. He closed out the thought. It would be bad luck. If you anticipated failure, you failed. He would not anticipate failure.

"How we feel personally doesn't matter," he said, hardening his voice. "We are soldiers. Our only objective is to win. Wait for my instructions."

He rose and walked off, and Khadija lay with her nails stabbing into her palms. Ballieu was losing his nerve, she thought. Or his judgment. He was going to wait and play the Americans' games while they sprang some sort of trap. It was stupid.

Above the sounds of the pool she could hear the constant clatter of dishes being cleared away and new dishes coming. Things to drink, with umbrellas and colored cherries on top. Ice cream. Sandwiches that were pushed away half eaten. Twenty-four hours a day Americans ate and drank while other people starved.

Four teenagers descended, laughing, on the chair Ballieu had abandoned. Fat Zionists, Khadija thought, the girls obscenely overflowing their bathing suits. The boys sniffed after them like dogs. One of the boys turned to leer at Khadija. The sweet desire to see all four of them with their brains splattered out rose inside her.

Khadija turned her face away. She had been born in a refugee camp and had grown up in guerrilla outposts in the Bekaa Valley. Her little brother had died in a Zionist raid on one of the camps. Khadija carried inside her own body pieces of shrapnel. Her mother had died in a failed attempt to blow up a diplomat's car. A heroine. Khadija had been fifteen when she first shouldered a rifle in her people's cause.

The soft and stupid youths beside her laughed again.

Splintered glass? It would be such an easy and unsuspicious way to slaughter a few pigs and the Stuart woman as well. Ballieu was mad not to kill her. Khadija wavered, drowning in her own anger.

Even if she could defuse the bomb and get the film tonight, she would have to depend on Ballieu to get it out of the country. She had no idea who his contacts were. She had been sent simply to help. Yet more and more it became apparent to her that Ballieu's judgment couldn't be trusted.

If he waited and they were captured, they would accomplish nothing. They would be fools, not martyrs. They would be held up for the world to laugh at.

She rose and walked angrily back into the lodge. Coming after a piece of film was all very well. She could see its endless value to her group and others. But she had expected more when she volunteered for this assignment. She had expected a bombing, a kidnapping—some chance to kill Americans.

Prowling down a side hall, she was forced to move aside for a long cart bearing a display of fruit. The two men wheeling it noticed something missing, stopped and conferred, then disappeared back through a distant door.

Khadija stared at the tiers of fruit cut into fancy shapes. Huge clumps of grapes, whole pineapples, and uncut melons sprawled around them. Her eyes lighted, lingering, on a thick-skinned melon the size of a man's head.

She could not force her eyes to move. Instinct, rather than a conscious effort to check, told her the hall was still deserted. Her face contorted. In a darting movement the side of her hand slashed out to cave in the side of the melon. Flesh and sticky juices oozed across her fingers.

She had no recourse against Ballieu's infernal waiting. But she wasn't going to content herself with a piece of film.

Every sort of sleight of hand performed, with coins or thimbles, ropes or cigarettes, cards—or film—brought into play a subtly different group of muscles. Channing felt the reminder of it throughout her hand as she held the film before her, flicked her fingers, and watched in the mirror for any telltale movement. Since morning she had executed the switch a thousand times, flawlessly. She had thought herself in peak condition because of her coin work, but she could feel muscles throughout her forearms pleading for rest.

She and Serafin had enjoyed a leisurely lunch from room service, and now she became aware she hadn't yet heard him leaving for the pool, which he adored. Stepping through the bath that connected their rooms, she found him sprawled across the bed with his chin in his hands. His face was toward the television, but she could tell by his expression that his thoughts were on nothing remotely connected to the images flickering there. A dark unhappiness pinched his features. Channing snapped off the TV and sat down next to him.

He seemed to anticipate her question even before she opened her mouth to speak.

"Why do you figure Mr. Yussuf was being so nice to me?" He rolled over and looked at her, and again she thought how his eyes were too old for his years. Yet this time they were haunted as well. "What was he going to use me for?" His forehead wrinkled.

Channing felt clumsy, unsure how to cancel out the self-doubt and betrayal she heard in his voice. Didn't she, too, feel betrayed by what Yussuf had been?

"He wasn't going to use you," she said, and the words came out harsher than she'd intended.

Serafin looked stubborn.

"Bullshit, Channing. I heard most of what those men said when they came to your house. He was rotten."

"So what? He still was capable of being a friend." She was snapping now, saying things she wasn't sure of herself because it was important that Serafin believe them. And she knew he'd forgive her brusqueness, even as she softened it. "Yussuf was nice to you because he liked you. You've got to believe that."

He squinted at her for a long minute, then sighed. "Yeah, maybe."

She could hear the hurt still lodged deep down, but the child in him became more cheerful.

"I'm hungry. You think we could get a piece of pie or something?"

"I thought you were going swimming. You'll sink like a rock."

"Yeah, maybe I oughta swim first." He slipped off the bed and gave her a grin. "Oh, say, Channing, don't worry about me when you've got things to do, okay? I already talked to Wilbur. Told him I was getting tired of the rat race and all this traveling. I said I was interested in finding out about hotel work when he had some time, and he said fine."

Two minutes later Serafin was out the door, whistling. Channing resumed her position in front of the mirror. She switched the film. She'd meet Ballieu tonight, and she felt ready.

She turned to observe a different angle and flexed her muscles to repeat the switch. Suddenly the smoothness of her movement was marred. She felt a tug. A piece of film veered and buckled, midway between her fingers and her sleeve. Channing stared, aghast, a sensation of coldness spurting through her pores.

The film had slid on into position, forced by the automatic movement of her fingers. But there had been a visible hitch. Something had happened.

She stared, not at her hand but at its reflection. It wasn't possible. What had she done wrong? She repeated the movements tensely, perfectly. No. It wasn't her. It couldn't have been. What else could have caused the slip?

Stripping off her jacket, she examined the sleeve and lining for a slub, a loose thread, anything. Nothing caught her attention. Dropping the jacket, she studied all edges of the film itself, with her eyes and with her fingers. Could there be a rough spot, brought out by practice or from some latent flaw in the film itself?

She became aware of the tension in her face, a straining throughout her body, and worse still, a pounding doubt.

What if it *had* been her? What if she wasn't equal to the task she had accepted?

She had buried her talent, turned her back on her Stuart heritage. Now, when all her training could count for something, she was suddenly unsure of herself. It seemed impossible that she herself could have glitched without knowing it, yet she relived that sickening sensation of the film snagging. She wanted to believe it had been something she could rectify, something that would never occur again if she discarded this jacket and used another piece of film. Yet what if it wasn't?

The sound of the telephone bulldozed the silence, flinging her thoughts aside and leaving a bare space.

"Come down two floors. I'll meet you at the elevator," said Ellery's voice.

"You're going to try to make Ballieu believe you need to be there when the film changes hands? You're going to lead us to it?"

Max circled Channing with a slack-jawed disbelief that tickled Ellery. They were in the listening post. As soon as Channing had made that call to Ballieu, Ellery had known he'd have to bring her here. With the bug on Ballieu's phone, either Max or Walker would have picked up what they believed was a new scent. Quick contact with Oliver had confirmed the wisdom of untangling things. Ellery had broken the news to the others before bringing her down to meet them. Ballieu was in his room right now, and Max and Walker were changing shifts.

"That's right," said Channing, answering Max's question. "And then I hope the rest of you are fast at doing what you do."

No reference to the switch she was there to perform. Ellery had told her Oliver didn't want that part mentioned. He saw her steal a glance to confirm she was playing it right. He nodded slightly.

Was he imagining it; or was there a strain around her mouth that hadn't been there before?

"Maybe I won't have to cramp my ass so much in front of this damned equipment, then," growled Walker. He was middle-aged, black, and perpetually disgruntled. Chewing an unlighted cigar, he sat hunched in front of a video screen that showed the door of Ballieu's room. His head was hooked to earphones. Various pieces of electronic gear were spread on the desk before him.

Ellery saw Channing taking in every detail: the equipment, the .38 tossed on the bed, the one Max was hiding under the expensive golf jacket he was shrugging into for a shift downstairs. Her eyes recorded it all with a single sweep.

"Hey, listen, it's tough being new." Max was recovering his footing. He slipped a hand under Channing's elbow and started to draw her along with him toward the door. "I've got this shift in the lobby in case Ballieu leaves his hole. But let me buy you dinner when I'm done. Bill can spell Walker, and I'll clue you in on how things usually work in a setup like this."

Ellery had to press his injured shoulder to curtail amusement at the look crossing Channing's face. With her free hand she reached beneath her elbow to flick Max's grip away with the tips of her nails.

"I generally buy men dinner," she said. "If I'm interested."

Max's jaw dropped. His gaze shot in question to Ellery's. His blue eyes started to narrow as his quick mind grasped at last that he'd been misled.

"I owe you one, pal," he murmured, nudging Ellery in the ribs in passing. He took his exit with an air of pretended injury.

Ellery crossed the room to look over Walker's shoulder. He'd give Channing a minute more to look at things, though she wouldn't be sharing the work in here.

"Anything new?" he asked.

"Not a thing." Walker fiddled with dials. "That other room Yussuf booked still looks empty."

The joke on Max already forgotten, Ellery ran the back of a knuckle across his lower lip and frowned with displeasure. Yussuf had made three reservations: one for himself; one for someone named Cardwell, which Ballieu had claimed; and one they'd assumed was for whoever was selling the film. If the seller hadn't shown up . . .

"I don't like it." Walker's words paralleled Ellery's thoughts. "Something's not right."

Ellery moved his head in slow agreement.

Several things weren't right. Yet he couldn't quite put his finger on what they all added up to. In addition, Oliver wanted a low profile here so they didn't spook Ballieu. One man had to be with the equipment all the time, to monitor and relay messages from Oliver, who'd set up down the road with a couple of men. That left just two of them to keep an eye on both Channing and Ballieu.

Last year Ballieu had gotten wind of a girl French intelligence had planted in his organization. Word was he'd gutted her like a pig.

Turning suddenly, Ellery looked at the woman who was temporarily his partner. She was standing at the window now, her arms crossed, hugging her shoulders. Oliver had been right. She wasn't a girl. She knew too much, watched things too closely for the label. But what kind of defense was magic against someone like Ballieu?

Channing felt him watching her in the same instant she realized her cheeks were wet. She'd been remembering the little girl in a bright pink dress who had died in her arms in that restaurant in Beirut. The scene and the feel of blood soaking into her blouse had returned to clutch at her even as she tried to avoid them.

The child's arms had been blown off at the shoulders, and in all the noise and confusion no one was paying any attention to her. Channing, dazed with seeing Tony's body, realizing he was dead, had held the whimpering child and kissed her forehead. It was all she knew to do. From the first she had known the child would die. She could feel the blood surging out. And she had felt so helpless. . . .

"Something wrong?" asked Ellery as he came to her side.

His presence took the sharp edge of the memory away.

"No. Yes."

She rubbed her forearm over her cheeks so he wouldn't see it was tears she was wiping away.

"Ellery, if it turns out I can't do this—if we fail—what happens?"

"We try to take the film by force. Maybe lose some people. Maybe it gets away."

She saw his mouth tighten.

"Several overseas intelligence sources have picked up rumors that some group, somewhere, plans to blow up an airport next week—location unknown. Forged passports may be what they're counting on to get them in. So we damn well better not let it get away. Why?"

Behind them, oblivious to their conversation, Walker stood up and tossed his earphones onto the desk.

"How about one of you spelling me for a while? My daughter's expecting a baby any day now. Want to go make a phone call. See how she's doing." He beamed suddenly, as though he did it all the time. "First grandchild."

Ellery waved agreement. Channing felt his sharpening alertness even though she could see no outward trace of it. This was her chance to do something for everyone who had died in that restaurant. But she had to be honest with Ellery. If she got her chance to switch the film and glitched again, his life would be in danger as well as her own.

"The film snagged," she said when the door had closed behind Walker. "Just before I came down here. I don't understand it. It's been going fine. I think it was a thread on my jacket. Or the film—a rough spot—"

"Are you sure?"

She watched the slow vibration of Ellery's throat. She heard the implication of his words: It might have been her.

"Not a hundred percent," she said grimly.

His attention flicked toward the radio equipment he'd promised to monitor. She could feel the pressure, feel him weighing this, feel his waning confidence in her even before he spoke.

"Jesus!"

Ten

"Had enough of the kid already, madam?"

Rundell's smugness, funneled through the telephone cable, did more to kick Channing's spirits back into order than any reasoning she'd done since leaving Ellery. It had to have been some flaw in materials, not her own skills, that had caused that hitch in the film. Ellery might have his doubts, but she didn't. Couldn't. She was urged ahead not only by her own drive, but also by a vision of Gramps urging her to prove herself. She lay back in the cool of her room, the phone to her ear.

"The 'kid' is no problem at all. But I need a card shaver, Rundell."

She could hear surprise in his second of silence. This wasn't what he'd expected.

"A card shaver, madam?"

"That's right. Has your hearing gone bad? I need it just as soon as you can get it."

She gave him the names of two sources. With a little luck he'd be able to get it today. If he expressed it out, it might arrive by midday tomorrow. Until then she'd just have to count on luck.

With a few crisp words Rundell hung up on her to do her errand. Too restless for anything else, Channing rose and began to practice with the pieces of film. She'd asked Ellery for a replacement, to eliminate any chance of the problem being a rough spot in the film. He'd said it was impossible. So with a card shaver, generally used for such unsavory purposes as marking a deck, she'd make sure the edges of the film were smooth. It was a chance, but rather than simply sitting down and whimpering, she'd take that chance.

"Something bothering you, Billy?"

Max swung cheerfully into place on the opposite side of the table where Ellery sat observing the pool scene. Ellery let Channing Stuart, reading in a lounge chair, slide into the edge of his vision.

"Yeah. The heat," he answered, filing away the fact that his face had betrayed his tension, if not its cause. This new turn—the fumble with the film—breathed on his back like a faceless presence.

If he pulled Channing, they'd have to bring in more help—FBI, try to capture Ballieu, risk a shoot-out, maybe never know who had stolen the film. If he didn't pull her, he might risk her life.

He had to decide what to do, report the incident to Oliver or trust her ability. The irony was that he was even wavering. He'd been against the whole idea of using her in the first place. Yet now he had started to sense not only her competence, but also how she was being driven to prove something to herself—to silence something in the past. He understood that need well enough, Ellery thought bitterly.

"It's a son of a bitch, isn't it?" asked Max, squinting at the sun and fanning his collar.

Ellery saw him check the pocket beeper that

would alert him if Ballieu left his room. It wasn't a perfect system, but Max and Walker couldn't risk showing up afterward every time Ballieu surfaced. Whoever had downstairs duty had to be in place at least part of the time.

"Walker seems kind of testy," said Ellery. "I offered to buy him a sandwich before he headed back up to relieve you, and he bit my head off."

"Pissed he didn't get that promotion to a desk job he'd been shooting for." Max raked a hand through his black curls and stretched comfortably, putting his legs out. "Doesn't like your style, either. Face it, Billy, you're so goddamn set on perfection, I've wanted to take a swing at you a time or two myself." His features drew back in a lazy smile. "Always wondered which one of us would come out the winner if I did."

Max signaled to a waiter and Ellery chuckled, coaxed from his somberness by Max's humor.

"Anything new on our man?" he asked, glancing across the pool to reassure himself Channing was still reading.

Max lit a cigarette. His expression tightened.

"Just that the man's endurance is frigging amazing. He was in one woman's room at the crack of dawn and just paid a visit to another who, reliable sources tell me, is a high-class hooker. Besides which he's been chatting up a brunette who'd give any man hot flashes *and* playing bridge with some old broad. Sure doesn't fit the profile of someone in his line of work, does it?"

Ellery felt the unpleasant breath at his back again.

"It could be a smoke screen. He could be trying to throw off anyone watching him. It could be he's making contact with one of them."

"He's sure as hell making contact," Max said with a leer.

"Have you sent in photos of the women to see if we've got anything on any of them?"

"C'mon, Ellery. The man works alone."

"Yeah. I guess."

"Buy you a beer?"

Ellery shook his head.

"I'll tell you," drawled Max, still stretched out to his full length, "listening to his activity's making me properly horny." He looked across the pool. "You think our Channing would accommodate? Assuming I make up for that fall on my ass you helped me take?"

Ellery kept his face perfectly clear of the irritation that swelled inside him at Max's crudeness.

"I couldn't say."

Max was looking at him closely now but wasn't getting satisfaction.

"You interested in her, Billy?"

"That would be fairly stupid, wouldn't it?"

Ellery's words sounded more clipped than he'd meant them to be. Max balanced a spoon between his two hands. His fingers were long and blunt with prominent knuckles.

"Getting mixed up with a woman's always stupid."

He sat up suddenly. The deceptive languidness of his manner vanished. His face looked strained.

"You ever have premonitions, Billy?"

"Hunches? I suppose so. Why?"

Max's eyes looked at empty air beyond Ellery's shoulder.

"I don't know. No reason. Only . . ." He shrugged, one hand lifting to rub at the back of his neck. "I keep having this feeling this is going to be my last time out."

Channing had thought to compose herself and lose herself in the anonymity of the main lounge before going on. Unfortunately Wilbur, the balding assistant manager, had spotted her as soon as she entered. Now, just as he was leaving, she saw Max coming toward her. Ellery must be elsewhere and Max in charge of watching her, she thought with annoyance. Baby-sitting or just making sure she didn't slip up?

"I like it. I definitely like it," Max said, leaning easily on the bar and eyeing her black magician's dress, the golden *kunjar* riding at its waist.

His gaze traveled up to the full pompadour that Channing knew gave her a different persona entirely. She could feel it happening when the hair went up and the dress went on. She became a Stuart. A conjurer. And tonight, if Ballieu showed up in response to her phone call, she was counting on the added powers that seemed to flow with that role.

"Looks like there's a fan who wanted to make sure he didn't miss your show."

Max flicked an eye, and Channing followed its direction to see Henri Ballieu settling in a few tables back from the stage.

"Well. If he's sitting down, maybe I don't need to worry about my neck."

She realized he hadn't understood her attempt at a joke. She felt antipathy toward Max. He seemed superficial, and that was not a quality she'd ever esteemed.

"Let me buy you one and we'll disappear where we don't attract notice," he said. "That mirror over there's two-way. We've got use of the office on the other side of it. What are you drinking?"

"A Virgin Mary—and I don't need another."

She turned to leave the room with him despite her personal feelings. They were coworkers, with more vested interest than most in getting along. Serafin was back in the dining room having a second dessert. She had time.

Max made a face at her words.

"You're not as clean-living as Billy, are you?"

"I'm working," she said pointedly.

Max had picked up a Scotch and water. He looked amused and hard to ruffle.

"Stick out like a bandaged thumb in this job if you don't at least pretend to drink," he said. "Didn't you learn that in training?"

He threw open the door to a small office. Across one wall a tinted window looked out onto the crowded lounge. Channing could see Ballieu. A woman was joining him. Channing weighed her answer, aware Max already had detected her hesitation.

"I didn't have training. I'm just the bait on this assignment. Because I knew Yussuf."

If he and Walker ever needed to rely on her, they ought to know that.

Max's eyebrows rose.

"Nervy. I guess I owe you an apology for that unsolicited two cents' worth." He waved around him. "Pretty nice setup, huh? The management thinks Walker and I are from the state liquor control, checking up on how they mind their p's and q's.

"Look, if you're coming into this thing cold, don't hesitate to ask for help if you need it—and don't take it to heart if Bill lights into you sometimes. He's a stickler for detail." Max hoisted his glass. "Great guy, but still a classic case of rich boy trying to redeem himself by playing cop."

Channing let her curiosity show before she could stop it. Max read it and grinned.

"Didn't you know? He's one of *the* Ellerys. Daddy made millions in real estate. Brother's a senator."

She felt annoyed, as though she'd betrayed Ellery in some way by revealing how little she knew about him.

"Well, speak of the devil," Max said cheerfully as the door opened.

Ellery sounded out of breath. His hair was disheveled.

"Search his room already?" asked Max.

"Just a once-over. We'll do the full treatment as soon as Channing starts her show. He tore out our bugs."

"Both of them?"

"Yeah. Awfully cautious or else he's suspicious."

Ellery's shoulders sloped as he sat on the edge of a desk.

"Goddamn ass-grabbing butcher." Max moved to the window, sipping his drink and peering out at Ballieu. "It'll spook him if we replace them," he said after a minute. "That means we're stuck with keeping tabs on the bastard by visual contact!"

"Looks like it." Ellery rubbed his hands together as if in thought. "This sure as hell isn't a place he'll carry a briefcase, and I don't see any other way to get a bug *on* him."

Max clinked the ice in his drink back and forth against the sides of his glass.

"How big are they?" asked Channing.

By the way their heads raised, she knew both men had all but forgotten her. Ellery came alert immediately, picking up the direction of her thoughts.

"They can come pretty small. You got an idea?"

"Could I get one into his wristwatch? Between the links of the band, maybe?"

Ellery was silent. Waiting. She sensed approval in the reaction—the first she'd felt from him. For an instant now she was truly part of the team.

"I'm going to do some close-up work in the audience. If I ask to borrow his watch, he'll think it's just a cover to set up a meeting."

Ellery's slow outward breath showed admiration as well as reluctance. Max let out a short whistle.

"Jesus, Billy. She's something!"

"I'd need to know what the watch is like before I try it." Channing was starting to feel the pressure of time. Fifteen minutes till she was due backstage, and not much time after that till she went on. "I'd need to see how it's built—where to put the thing. I'd need to practice."

Ellery seemed to think for a second and then, without speaking, snatched Max's glass up and was out the door. A moment later, through the window, he came into view strolling in Ballieu's direction.

"What—?"

Channing let her question die. She had moved to the window and watched with Max.

Ellery pretended to lose his grip on the glass, which spilled onto Ballieu's table. Ellery bent, apparently apologizing, and summoned a waiter. Ballieu's hands pantomimed an irritated "It's okay." He moved to a neighboring table.

"That's Billy," said Max with a grin. "Nerve clear up to the old—well, you get the drift."

Channing scarcely nodded. Ellery was making an exit into the hall. Time was precious. She hurried to join him.

There were couples drifting toward the lounge to find a place for the floor show, a Latin tamale with a drink in her hand and three men following her. Channing dodged around them. She and Ellery fell into step together, walking quickly and like strangers.

"It's a Rolex," Ellery said. "Metal expansion band pretty much like this, if you want to use it."

He slipped a cheaper watch from his wrist and Channing took it, all in one smooth movement.

"I'll get what you need and drop it off in your dressing room in a couple of minutes."

There was no time for more. They split off like two people going opposite ways in a marching band. Yet Channing felt a sudden synchronization between them.

A moment later she was through the door to her dressing room. Serafin stood in front of the mirror. He wore pants and a cutaway jacket, borrowed from a dining room waiter with the explanation that his own had been lost in transit. Channing wondered briefly how many untruths she'd tell in behalf of him and Ellery before she was finished. Serafin turned. He was clearly excited.

"I've got everything set up for you, Channing. I've rolled all your silks and have your glycerin out." He noticed the watch she was starting to test with her fingers. "What're you going to do?"

"Practice something new that I'm trying tonight. Could you go to the coffee shop and get me a ginger ale? I'm really thirsty."

It was crazy. She half feared if he watched her practicing, he'd somehow guess what she was up to. In any case, he couldn't be here when Bill Ellery arrived with the bug.

As Serafin reached for the doorknob a swell of caring rose in her throat that made speech difficult. This wasn't how she'd meant things to be. He deserved better than what she was giving. She'd never been much good at apologies, any more than she'd been at flirting or cooking or a dozen other things most women took for granted. Maybe she'd never been very good at saying what she was feeling, either.

"Serafin." She hoped he'd be able to see through the clumsiness of her words. "What kind of pet would you like to have when we get home?"

Eleven

Applause was sounding, and Ballieu joined in politely. By his calculation the magic act would be next.

"They have such marvelous entertainment here, don't you think?" asked Mildred Farrow with a timid uncertainty that grated on Ballieu's nerves.

Her hair was feathered back, and she wore a white dress that looked rather nice on her. Ballieu smiled and let the back of his hand brush hers as he reached for the snifter of brandy that sat between them.

Almost from the beginning his organization had recognized the advantage he offered for blending into settings like this, where money and imperialist tastes went hand in hand. In the first place he was not afraid of being looked at, whereas others panicked. In the second he understood the wisdom of making the little gestures, displaying the charm and playing the games that kept those around him unwary. Most important, of course, was his blondness, and the ease with which he could wear expensive suits. The belligerent, the unkempt, the wild-eyed would be caught at this game. Ballieu had never been caught.

"And now, ladies and gentlemen, an act whose

name says it all. She's—the Magic Lady," the emcee announced.

Ballieu set his glass down abruptly and looked at Mildred Farrow.

"Forgive me. I didn't know this would affect me. My wife . . . my wife was very fond of magic. I think I'd like to see this alone."

He'd timed the move perfectly, and as he remained seated, Mildred Farrow got the message that she was the one expected to leave.

"Oh . . . of course," she whispered.

Ballieu sat back. Black velvet curtains were parting on stage. In front of them, at center, sat an empty, thronelike chair. It was high-backed, with plumes on the top and velvet upholstery. Suddenly smoke puffed out and a woman sat in the midst of it —all in an instant. Ballieu found himself tensing.

The cleverness with which she'd materialized was distracting. She held herself like a column of ebony in her long black gown. Her eyes seemed to search him out and met his without flinching. Fire flashed from her fingertips. A wand appeared.

Anger rose like bile in Ballieu's throat. What did she know about the deal that Yussuf had struck? Was it really in jeopardy?

A boy in a cutaway coat stepped from the wings to hand the Stuart woman a large square of red silk. She performed in silence, accompanied by music.

Across the room, Khadija was also watching. Her hair was down. She looked like any other American woman on the prowl. Ballieu hoped she did not arouse too much interest. He might need her. More than that, he hoped she was able to lay aside her zeal in favor of alertness.

Onstage, in her glittering black dress, the magician had passed from tricks with scarves to filling a bucket with coins that rained out of nowhere. Next she began to work with foot-wide silver rings that linked together. At last she tossed the rings to her assistant and came to the front of the stage where she bowed to warm applause.

"And now I'll ask some of you in the audience to assist me," she said, starting down.

Her eyes were on Ballieu again. He watched a light flicker in them. They were hypnotic. Challenging. Dark with a strange and unleashed boldness Ballieu thought could make her careless.

To his surprise she turned toward a woman in the audience.

"Do you have a compact?" she asked.

She borrowed a five-dollar bill from a man at another table, made it vanish out of her hand, and reappear in the compact the woman was holding.

At last she began to make her way toward him. Ballieu could feel a magnetic thread connecting them. Her hips were narrow. The sheath of her short J-shaped knife swayed exotically. An absurd affectation, making a trinket of a knife designed to kill and maim, Ballieu thought.

"Now if I could borrow a wristwatch," she said, stopping by his table. "You'll lend me one, won't you, sir? You look like a good sport."

Ballieu had not anticipated she'd be fool enough to focus every eye in the room on him. He didn't like it. There was only one safe way to play the situation.

"Of course," he said smoothly, stripping it from his wrist.

His eyes never broke their connection, and hers never wavered. She held out her hand. Her voice dropped to a whisper.

"Yussuf set a trap. I can get you out. Terrace bar—after the second show."

She turned toward a nearby table, her wrist flicking smartly over as she placed his watch in front of a gray-haired woman.

"Now, will you just cover this with your hand? You're sure it's a watch you're covering?"

When the woman in the audience removed her hand, Ballieu saw his watch had been exchanged for a book of matches. The watch appeared in another man's pocket. The Stuart woman made jokes about timing three-minute eggs with a pack of matches and lighting a pipe with a watch, and everyone laughed.

Ballieu waited, wondering what she'd meant about a trap. He'd expected blackmail, not this hint of complicity.

She returned his watch. Ballieu felt a pain stab his belly and reached into his pocket to unwrap another peppermint.

What was her game that she approached him so boldly?

He crumpled the candy wrapper and rolled it between his palms, thinking.

* * *

"Nothing," said Ellery bitterly, standing at the center of Ballieu's closet and surveying again the items of clothing they'd searched seam by seam and thread by thread. Using one side of the door as an anvil, he pounded the heel back onto one of Ballieu's shoes, which he'd been inspecting.

"That's every inch," said Walker, replacing the air-conditioning grid he'd just removed.

They'd been in the room for almost an hour and found no trace of money, no clue who might be selling the film to Ballieu.

"Maybe he's paying in something he can carry on him," said Walker. "A draft on a Swiss bank. Diamonds. Even shoved up his ass, maybe."

"Yeah, maybe," echoed Ellery.

His shoulder itched from not being able to wash it. Or maybe from healing. He was tired and thought fleetingly how good it would feel to stretch out with a drink and let down a little. But already his mind was moving on downstairs to where Channing would be finishing her act about now. There'd been no message from Max, who was watching her, so she must be okay.

"Let's clear in case he comes up between shows," he said, looking at the clock built into the room's TV cabinet.

They returned to the listening post. Walker slid in under the headphones, twisted dials, and gave a sudden thumbs-up sign.

"Listen," he said, indicating a second pair of earphones. "I think she got it on him—I can hear voices. But either the damn thing's got static or he's crinkling paper."

"Candy," said Ellery, listening a minute. "When I spilled that drink to get a look at his watch, he was unwrapping candy."

Strange anomaly in a man who made war on innocent people.

Channing was to have scheduled her meeting with Ballieu for after the second show. Ellery knew she'd hold up her end, but he wasn't sure about Ballieu. He decided to go down early and get in position, just to be safe.

The terrace bar was the noisiest of Palacio Sol's late-night action spots. It was open-air, with a tile floor and a mariachi band.

Under lantern light a few couples bumped along on a postage-stamp-size dance floor: a trim older duo who executed their intricate steps flawlessly and without expression. A pair of lovers. A fat retiree hanging on to a girl with long black hair and a sulky mouth. Channing stood for a minute, watching, screened by a piece of grillwork that held pots of geraniums. Her heart beat so deep in her chest and so coldly, it was hard for her to get her breath.

She tried to pick out details that would reassure her. Ellery sat hunched above a glass, appearing indifferent to the scene around him. Walker was at a table laughing with two young women. Henri Ballieu sat a little apart, in the shadow of a low wall. Alone. She felt strangled by sudden hate of what he stood for, but along with the feeling came an unexpected and numbing fear.

What if she couldn't do it?

What if she couldn't look in his eyes and hide what she felt and make him believe her story?

But she was a Stuart. It was time for her to perform.

Squaring her shoulders, she began to walk toward Ballieu's table. His head raised almost at once, as though he could smell her.

He looked at her as she sat down. He didn't speak. Neither did Channing. Around them the sights and sounds blurred together, fireworks exploding in bursts of noise and color. She could feel the air between them throb as they challenged each other. The hate she felt for him flowed into her, molding her and giving her the ruthlessness of the role she played.

"I worked for Yussuf," she said boldly. "I know about Marinka, Colón—everything."

She waited to let the names sink in. His only response was the faint shrinking of his pupils.

"I've taken over his network," she said. "I want to be on good terms with your organization. Yussuf was setting a trap for you, but there's a way around—"

So swiftly she didn't have time to flinch, his hand moved, pinning her wrist to the table.

"Disengage the timing device."

His words were the glint of a knife edge, a threat that need not be articulated. Channing's breath stalled. She didn't know what he was talking about.

"I can't."

Instinctively she knew it was the thing to say. She

got her balance back. Ballieu's hand pressed harder against her wrist.

"What do you mean you can't?"

The pieces fell into place before her. This explained why he was waiting.

"The timing device was Yussuf's idea," she said. "I can't undo it. But I can see that you get out with the film. If I'm not there when you pick it up, you won't walk away."

It was someone else speaking in her voice, someone as coldly composed as Ballieu himself. The man across from her sat back. At the edge of her vision she saw Bill Ellery do the same, as if he'd been about to rush them.

"I don't like threats," said Ballieu. "Or blackmail."

"Which is why you killed Yussuf?"

There was a wine bottle on the table. And two glasses. She reached and filled one, uninvited.

"I'm making a peace offering, not threatening. I'm not asking a cent except what you owed Yussuf for setting up the deal."

"Why?" There was no indication at all in his face of what he was thinking.

"Didn't I make it clear enough? I want to keep doing business with you."

He hadn't decided yet what to make of her story. That was how she read it. Which meant, she told her knotted nerves, that she had a chance.

"The magician thought he could ambush me?"

His eyes were pale and chill. He was pretending unconcern. Or was he pretending?

Channing gave a knowing look. She rose.

"Let's say he expected to sell the film twice. To you, and then when you were out of the way, to another buyer. Of course, if you don't want my help, you can always try to shoot your way out."

She turned. He made no move to stop her. He wasn't biting, and her mouth felt dry with worry.

A few tables over, Ellery was tossing a couple of peanuts into his mouth, slouching toward the door without so much as a look in her direction. Channing set her teeth, thinking of an airport sprayed with blood if Ballieu got what he wanted.

She looked at him across her shoulder, adopting the same careless tone she'd used in their whole conversation.

"Think about it."

She walked briskly back to her dressing room. Her determination not to think Ballieu might be behind her, or what he might do if her story didn't offer the protection Oliver Lemming thought it would, held her erect. This was war. She understood that now. She'd understood it sitting there across from Ballieu.

She slid into her dressing room, closed the door, and sagged against it with relief. Sensing a presence, she snapped herself back together. Her eyes jerked open. Bill Ellery lounged against her dressing table, one leg hooked over the corner. She started forward, but he intercepted her, catching her shoulders.

She felt his tension. And his unvoiced question.

"I don't know if it worked. He didn't take me up on the deal." Her voice lacked the steadiness she was used to, but she knew a part of the reason was anger. If a few men like Ballieu could plunge the whole world into chaos, then by God a few like her and Ellery could make it sane again.

"Learn anything?"

"Yes. There's some sort of timing device. He asked me to disarm it."

"A time bomb in reverse." He let his breath out slowly and stepped back. "That's why he hasn't run. Yussuf must have put the film in some sort of vault they can't open."

He smelled of soap and shaving cream. Channing could see the outline of his Adam's apple.

"Not right here in the hotel." She found that possibility too farfetched.

"No. Somewhere near here. If we can find out where, that's our ace in the hole."

She didn't understand and must have shown it, for his mouth began to relax in the first traces of a smile.

"You can make things vanish; I can take bombs apart. Are you okay?"

Ellery knew he shouldn't have touched her just now. It hadn't been necessary. But she'd looked drained when she'd come through that door, and then immediately had bluffed, pretending she wasn't. He wished he wasn't starting to see so many sides of her and that she hadn't performed so well. It was making things harder.

She had nerve enough for any three people, but nerve wasn't enough. You had to know when to be scared. She hadn't been trained . . . didn't have a gun . . . would, he was starting to feel, equate backing down with failure. And her life was in his hands.

"You're doing a damn good job," he said.

He wondered whether she still dreamed about the doctor in Beirut.

"Let's call it a day," he said abruptly.

Ballieu prowled his room lifting pictures off the wall and looking in lamp shades. The people watching him would have searched his room in his absence. The question was whether they'd been foolish enough to leave more of their electronic bugs.

He finished his circuit. Nothing. They were smart enough to realize that if he'd torn out the last ones, he'd search again. They were taking care not to scare him away. They were counting on him to lead them to the film itself. He'd disappoint them.

His only worry was over the woman who'd met him in the bar. Could she be telling the truth? The magician Yussuf had no political loyalties, only a love of money. He would not have been above such a trick. And the woman herself seemed fearless. It was possible.

The phone rang bringing him to instant alertness. No one should be calling him here. A pulse of high-frequency sound to rupture his brain? No, they wanted him to lead them to the film. Perhaps it was only the desk, or one of the women he'd met. He answered.

"Don't say a word," a male voice cautioned. It was the seller's voice. "Your watch has ears. The woman who put it there is working for their side."

Ballieu held a minute in disbelief, then slammed

the receiver down savagely. Bitch. Cunning American liar. Was it possible she could have done it right before his eyes?

He ripped his watch from his wrist, bent the segments apart, and saw the evidence. His fingers reached out to destroy it, then pulled back as he smiled.

Twelve

Ballieu slept late and awoke with a sense of tranquillity that seemed to drag at his body. For the first time in years he had dreamed of the village where he had been born. Light dancing as it could only in the sun-drenched lands of the southern Mediterranean. Lushness. Colors. The wavering call from the minaret that, though he couldn't remember a time when he hadn't scorned Allah as a fairy tale fit only for children, nevertheless had soothed like music. The clear and lingering images haunted even as they beckoned to him. He could almost smell the dust in the streets. From somewhere inside him there trickled an unknown rivulet that he recognized as fear.

Shaking off the torpor that was pulling at him, Ballieu sat up. He ran a forearm over his face and found it bathed in cold sweat. Absurd. Ridiculous. There was nothing wrong with him. Nothing that mattered, anyway. He flung the sheets from him and, with cool and practiced discipline, brought all the resources of his mind to bear on the problems at hand.

So the woman who had told him she was taking over Yussuf's business was nothing more than a U.S. spy. Ballieu pulled open the draperies and examined his fingernails. A pity. There was something fascinating about her. Some element he had always found more prevalent in danger than in women.

Ballieu narrowed his eyes and found he could recall the exact shade of her hair and the look of challenge in her eye. He had always wanted to bed a U.S. agent. He wondered what sort of trick this was that she was playing on him. The seller would call at 10:21, and Ballieu would learn more then.

He looked at his watch with the treacherous implant that might have spoiled all his plans. Now that he knew of its presence, he would make good use of it, just as he might make good use of the woman, for his own amusement if not as a matter of safety. Ballieu placed the watch carefully on the sink and, with a smile gliding across his lips, stepped into the shower.

After his shower, naked, he examined his body before a mirror. The scars left by surgery three years ago were almost lost amid older ones—from a mortar attack, a comrade's treachery, and a bullet received when he was very young and less efficient than he was now. Those lines, and the firmness of his body itself, proved he was a soldier. The muscles across his torso and belly were taut and flat.

He turned and began the course of calisthenics he did almost daily. Punishing sit-ups; push-ups; the leaping, twisting, turning movements of attack and escape. Lastly he brought his locked fists crashing against the part of his body where it would be softest, the spot in his belly. Surviving the pain would make him stronger. He drew up, gasping.

Perhaps when he finished this mission, he would become a training officer. He would handpick a few likely candidates who already had proved themselves and teach them the tactics and discipline at which he excelled.

For now it was time to go downstairs for two phone calls. For the first, from the man who was selling the film, he would make sure his watch and its cargo were safely deaf inside the phone book.

The second call he intended to be overheard.

It was still too early for the large swimming pool to be crowded. From a distance Ellery could see Channing pulling herself through the water with strong, even strokes. He felt a momentary irritation. Getting no answer when he'd called her room had made him uneasy. The concern had increased when he didn't see her on his first pass through the lodge.

"Nice morning," he said as she hit the side and shook the water out of her eyes.

He'd forgotten the impact her body had in the splashes of orange that made up her swimwear. Droplets of water were sliding down the curve of her breasts. He bent and offered a hand to haul her out. She hesitated.

Vulnerable? Ellery wondered. Or did she just resent him? She put her hand in his and he noted the startling strength in her fingers. He pulled her out in silence. Behind her Serafin was splashing gracelessly but exuberantly down the length of the pool.

"Next time let me know where you'll be before you set out in the morning," said Ellery as mildly as he could. "I'm supposed to be watching your back, remember?"

She nodded, a little short-winded from the vigor of her workout, and picked up a towel she'd left on a nearby chair.

"You don't swim, Ellery? You have the build of a swimmer."

She was all briskness, toweling her hair.

Was it simply a question, or was she wondering if he was armed? Ellery nudged his open collar back just enough for her to see the bulky bandage it concealed.

"Souvenir of Ballieu," he said. "The night he killed Sam and Yussuf."

He'd hoped it would make her cautious. He wasn't prepared for the change that came over her face. He saw fear in it—not fear for herself but fear for him.

Ellery swore silently. Just her overdue confrontation with their shared mortality, he told himself. He looked away. Serafin had climbed out of the pool and was coming toward them.

"Think I'll go have some more pancakes," he announced to Channing. "Over there so you can see I'm not snatched, huh? Let you two talk. How you doin', Ellery?"

Channing gritted her teeth. She started to speak but spotted a waiter bearing a large salad and a pot of coffee.

"Is that the Caesar salad?" she called. "I'll have it over there."

"That's breakfast?" Ellery grimaced, shifting the foil-wrapped candy box and folded-up newspaper he held under one arm.

"Why not?"

She shrugged into an oversize shirt that hid most of her curves. Ellery wondered how she got freckles on her arms without having them anywhere else.

"There's an egg in it, and fresh greens, which I miss when I'm traveling," she said. "The garlic's hard on the breath, but I wasn't figuring on kissing you, Ellery."

She had a habit of talking while she moved. She was already halfway to the table where the salad had been delivered.

"Enough to curdle my stomach," muttered Ellery.

She eyed him as he followed her.

"Are we supposed to be seen together?"

"Can't be avoided completely. People get together at places like this. Ballieu can think I'm an admirer."

He sat down at right angles to her, the folded-up newspaper on the table in front of him and pointed carefully out. She had noticed the lavish candy box with its red satin bow. He started to hand it to her but was interrupted by a white-haired couple stopping beside them.

"You did the magic act, didn't you?" said the man. "You were wonderful!"

Ellery let himself fade out a little, taking another look at the surroundings, alert for anything amiss. When he tuned back in, the couple was departing. They looked comfortable together, as though they had been that way for a long time. Ellery had a brief sense of a gap in his life that he didn't want to identify.

Channing was looking slightly embarrassed, yet pleased, at the recognition.

"What's the attraction?" asked Ellery. He had poured himself a cup of coffee and held it between his palms.

"That magic has for people?" Her eyes were thoughtful as she looked out over the pool. "We need our illusions, I guess. Gramps said we all need to believe there are things we can't explain. It gives us hope. It makes us feel less hemmed in by our ideas of what's possible and what isn't."

For a moment Ellery felt himself drawn into what she was saying. He shook himself free.

"As long as the illusions stay onstage," he said.

It broke her mood and she looked at him in challenge.

"We all do sleight of hand, Ellery. Inside our heads. We hide things that matter to us from the people around us—even from ourselves sometimes. I do it. You do it. Maybe even Ballieu does, God knows!"

He'd never thought about it that way, and he didn't want to. He slid the candy box toward her.

"Oliver wants you to have this. Careful opening it."

Her fingertips poised on the edges of it, as though they could see through. As though she suddenly recognized whatever was inside wouldn't match the pretty wrapping.

This time her face didn't betray her as she cracked the lid and saw the five-shot .38, somewhat smaller than his, that was wedged inside. She closed the box and shoved it back at him.

"I've got a knife."

"It's easier to pull a trigger. More removed."

Even though they were whispering, he made his voice harsh. He could feel the anger mounting inside her as they sat there in the warm morning sun amid innocent surroundings facing the very opposite of innocence that the gun represented. He'd had the same reaction sometimes.

Something else pushed out of him. A rage to get through to her. He leaned forward.

"It's a war," he said. "Don't you understand? Unless we want it to burn up the whole world someday, our only hope is to stop the generals."

Her mouth barely moved.

"I don't want to kill anybody!"

"You think I do? If I wanted to run around rubbing out people and setting up coups, I'd work for the CIA. I like what this department stands for—sanity, reason, cooling problems down instead of whipping them up—but it doesn't work against people like Ballieu."

He pulled back, frustrated at how much he'd let spill out. His philosophy wasn't any of her damned business. She was supposed to follow orders. The silence between them crackled. She made no move to retrieve the box, and he knew he couldn't force her to take the gun. She wasn't a regular agent.

A part of him admired the force of her conviction even as it angered him. After a good sixty seconds or more, she dipped into one of her shirt pockets and produced the wristwatch she'd borrowed from him the previous night.

"Here. I forgot to return this."

He recognized it was a gesture of peace.

"No problem." His words sounded stiff. Reluctantly he reached into a pocket of his trousers and displayed an old gold railroad watch to prove it really was no problem.

Amusement started up around her mouth. She was as mercurial as hell. The last kind of personality that ought to be in work like this. And she didn't care what he thought of her.

"Compulsive, aren't you, Ellery?"

The words were gently teasing, and he found himself responding to them. He felt sheepish.

"Belonged to my grandfather."

He let the watch turn on its chain, watching it instead of the woman beside him.

"Great old guy. A bricklayer. Only one in the family who didn't think I was a total screwup."

He was sorry at once that he'd said it. Her tone was light.

"Is that why you never let down, Ellery? Are you still trying to prove yourself?"

But Ellery didn't answer. He'd gone alert. A girl with long black hair was arranging herself in a chair beside the pool. He didn't like the fierceness with which her eyes had fixed on Channing. It triggered something in his mind—Max's comment about Ballieu flirting with women. This one looked familiar . . . the dance floor last night during Channing's meeting with Ballieu. There was probably nothing to it, but neither was there any point in taking chances.

Removing a pack of cigarettes from his pocket, he positioned it carefully. The faint clicking of the camera inside was camouflaged by the snap of his lighter. When he brought his attention back to the table, Channing Stuart was watching him closely. He wondered what she'd seen—or guessed.

She didn't ask anything, and he didn't answer. Walker had just come through the door to the main lodge and was scratching his head, a signal to come to the listening post.

Ellery hadn't wanted to include her in this meeting. Channing had sensed it when he'd first tensed at the table out there beside the pool. What had changed his mind? Concern for her safety? Fairness?

He'd told her to go ahead so they didn't look like Siamese twins—and to take her salad. She'd dropped Serafin off in their room and come directly to the listening post. She set her empty bowl aside just as Ellery entered.

"What's up?" he asked.

Walker was at the equipment, a sodden cigar hanging from his mouth. He'd answered Channing's conversational overtures with grunts.

"We've hit pay dirt," he said. "Ballieu's back in his room, but he made two calls from a lobby phone right before I came hunting you."

"Smart," said Ellery, leaning a hand on the table that held the equipment.

"Uh-huh." Walker's sour expression took on tinges of satisfaction. "But wait'll you hear what we've got!"

He reached toward a tape recorder. Before he could flip it on, there was a flushing sound in the bathroom. Max came out. His response to Bill's questioning look was a wan but rakish grin.

"Montezuma sneaked over the border last night. It's keeping me close to the porcelain. I'm holding the fort up here, and Walker's doing the legwork."

Ellery looked more harried than amused.

"For chrissake. That happened to you in Rome."

"Happens to him anywhere," drawled Walker. "Didn't you know? Get Max six states away from where he was born and his plumbing goes out."

Channing decided there might be a likable side to Walker. Max looked a little rumpled and not quite his teasing self.

"Hey, I'll be all right. I've got some medicine for it."

He motioned irritably to the tape recorder. Walker started it, and the voice of Henri Ballieu filled the room.

"What you need will be in my room tonight. Pick it up while I'm away—"

There was a clicking sound, a receiver being put down. Max was holding up a hand for silence. The next sounds, distorted eerily by their passage through the bug in his watch, were those of coins dropping into a slot and the musical notes of telephone buttons.

"We have to talk," said Ballieu.

The voice on the other end was indistinguishable. Ballieu spoke again.

"In the canyon. Eleven-forty tonight. There's a rock shaped like a cat about three hundred meters off the road."

Walker turned off the tape. The four who had

been listening were plummeted into silence. Channing felt a pleased quickening of her blood. She had planted the bug. She had gotten them this information.

"Looks like he bought Channing's story," said Walker.

To Channing's surprise he even gave her a wink.

Ellery was nodding.

"We're going to need more people."

"Can't get 'em, Billy." Max aimed a breezy pat at Ellery's shoulder in passing. "All the spares are tied up on something in Florida."

Walker rewound the tape.

"Also under budget items, the patch to Oliver keeps fading in and out."

"Goddamn," said Ellery, swerving to look in the back of a receiver-transmitter. "Got a match?"

While Ellery tinkered with the radio Max ducked in front of a mirror and combed his hair.

"Here's how we'll have to do it, Billy. I'll follow Ballieu. Walker can search his room and keep an eye out for whoever shows up there. You man things in here."

A dial at the front of the radio sprang to life again under Ellery's prodding.

"I'll follow Ballieu," said Ellery.

Max's comb stopped. The humor slipped from his face.

"Wait just a damned minute. Just because you think you walk on water—" He broke off, seized by a pained expression, and hastened back to the bathroom.

"Goddamn," said Ellery again.

Channing could see the concern etched into his face. The reservations Yussuf had made ran through tomorrow night. And Ballieu hadn't contacted her.

"Couldn't I help out tonight?" she offered. "Shouldn't whoever follows Ballieu out to that rock have some kind of backup?"

"Too risky," said Ellery. "And you have to be onstage. We need everything to look normal."

Walker favored her with a baleful glare, all cordiality forgotten. "We're used to playing shorthanded. Won't be anything different."

She was still window dressing, relegated to the fringes with nothing to do but wait for the card shaver to arrive. And practice.

Ellery went to lean against the bathroom door. "Hey, Max. I'm leaving my camera on your desk. Shore yourself up and get shots of the women you've seen with Ballieu. It may be a long shot, but let's get some film out to Oliver for a background check."

"All first-rate, Mama. You want to try?"

The man with the van tossed a Uzi Model B toward Khadija, who caught the automatic assault weapon by its grip and checked its mechanism. They were on a remote stretch of highway, parked well off the shoulder. The hood to Khadija's rented car was up, as well as the trunk lid. It looked as though the van had stopped to help. In the space of three minutes they had loaded eight weapons and several cases of ammunition clips into her trunk.

Besides the Uzis there were two AR-15s equipped with night scopes. Enough to deal with any problems that might arise when they picked up the film. Enough selection for any contingency, all arranged in advance. She had to acknowledge Ballieu had planned well on this part.

The weapons dealer, sent to the rendezvous by one of the cells that was helping them, shoved a false floor into the trunk to cover the merchandise. It was very innocent-looking—carpeted, even. Khadija had had her orders of the color and model of car she was to rent. The man she was dealing with and the people who had sent him had no idea how her purchase was to be used. That was the only safe way. Deal only with your own kind. No questions, no chance of betrayal—even under torture.

Her trunk slammed closed. The entire transaction had taken less than six minutes. Khadija walked quickly around her car and lowered the hood. Inside the car she rocked her foot, in its high-heeled sandal, down on the gas.

She had been right about the Stuart woman. An American spy. Yet still Ballieu was doing nothing. He made excuses . . . insisted the woman might be useful. He could not know what he was doing. She was very glad she had met him . . . glad she had destroyed all the myths.

Khadija pressed harder on the gas, keeping the car just under the legal limit as she drove through the shimmering heat of midday. By the time she got back to the resort, it would be time for lunch. It would be time for the Zionist teenagers to gather round their trough.

It would be time for the Stuart woman to eat. And drink.

Thirteen

"Perhaps you would care to lunch with me?"

Ballieu had appeared behind her so utterly without noise or warning that Channing jumped. She was in the lobby, on her way to change and meet Serafin, who had scampered ahead. There were people all around. Yet she had to fight a chill. It angered her.

She could see Ballieu's satisfaction at startling her. Yet relief shot through her.

"So, you've decided to talk," she said quietly.

He had taken the bait. She tried to will her blood back to normal speed. It ran with bitter elation.

"Why not?" said Ballieu. "What you said last night had a certain interest. Unfortunately . . ."

Hooking a strand of her hair around his finger, he exerted just the slightest pressure. He smiled, and to Channing's sudden shock there was, underneath his subtle move to intimidate, underneath the cold calculation, something that seemed to glitter on the edge of carnal flirtation.

"Unfortunately I'm not entirely sure I trust you."

With a moue of false apology he released her. He was watching for her reaction. Channing kept her face impassive.

"We're even, then, aren't we?" she said.

She thought what passed through his eyes was

anger. She stepped back and tossed her hair. If she made this too easy, Ballieu might grow suspicious. She tried to fathom a mind like his and couldn't. Just as she hadn't been able to reconcile what Yussuf had been in reality with the man she'd known, she thought.

The recollection of Yussuf became, in a twisting way, an inspiration.

"All right, lunch," she said. "But first I want Yussuf's tape back. It has sentimental value."

Ellery would be starting in soon, judging by his pattern. He'd been out by the pool, playing shuffleboard while she and Serafin alternately splashed in the water and read in the smidgen of shade to be found. She hoped he might be alert enough to see what was happening and delay a little, maybe come in by another entrance.

"Why don't we go to my room and get it now?" Ballieu suggested. "Perhaps you'll demonstrate the trick that's on it?"

A trap had opened at her feet. She had to play this out with him, yet Ellery's warning never to go off alone with him closed down all the other functions of her brain. And Ballieu was smiling at her. He'd already said he didn't trust her. He was giving her rope. Considering the stakes they were playing for, and his experience, he'd undoubtedly started to catalog faces and details around him—noticed Ellery. She was supposed to be the Dragon Lady, so she'd play the role.

"My bodyguard wouldn't like that," she said. Her vague and brazen smile echoed the same note of near flirtation he had struck. She saw him suck that particular fact in under the hoods of his eyes, and she felt clamminess creeping over her. Concentrate on the matter at hand. Her comeback had been a good one. Besides sounding in line with the part she was playing, it might give an inkling of how much he observed.

"The brown-haired fellow you had breakfast with this morning," he said, taking a narrow brown cigarette from a case in his pocket and lighting it. It was a volley in some game they played, and Channing could swear he was enjoying it.

"No. He's . . . an admirer." She willed a wider smile. "I see no reason to give up amusements just because I'm working, do you, Ballieu? Why don't you leave the tape at the front desk for me? If it's there when I come down, I'll have lunch with you."

His eyes had narrowed, yet they were glittering with something like enjoyment.

"A pledge of good faith," he said. "What time and where shall we meet?"

Channing hoped Ballieu's watch was picking this all up and that Walker or Max would get the details to Ellery. She dared not try to find him herself.

"Don't be late," she said when they'd made the arrangements. "I hate to wait."

She walked toward the elevators.

Walker came out in Bermudas and a garish sun hat just as Ellery was about to leave his lounge chair to follow Channing. Shambling along, unrepentantly knock-kneed, Walker unwrapped a cigar. He tossed the crumpled cellophane aside, landing it neatly inside the spread pages of the newspaper Ellery had been reading. Ellery waited, looked down, and saw there was a note inside.

So Ballieu had made an overture, he thought when he'd read it. This was the break they'd been waiting for, maybe. They'd sent in an amateur, and she'd turned the trick for them. Why the hell did his temples suddenly feel as if someone had threaded a ski pole between them?

He was worried. Things were moving too easily. Or maybe they were moving exactly as they should when a plan went well. Maybe he was losing his perspective because of Channing.

He couldn't let that happen. He wouldn't be any good to either one of them if he did. He wouldn't be any good to the department. He flipped a page of the paper and came face-to-face with a photograph of his brother, Reid, and two other senators.

Jesus Christ, he thought angrily. Here he was up to his ass in proverbial alligators, and Reid was heading up Be Kind to Animals Week. Not literally, of course. It was some committee for preservation of historic buildings. All the same, it seemed characteristic of the parallel there'd always been between them.

Reid overachieving without even drawing a breath; Ellery sweating whether he could even bring off a job. Reid walking in with no experience and being made editor of his college paper; Ellery spending three months on an essay for a contest and tying for fourth place. Reid could dazzle any woman he wanted. Probably even one as bright as Channing. But none of that mattered now, and he was a jerk to be thinking about it.

Twenty minutes remained till Channing's appointment for lunch. A little under eleven hours till Ballieu's meeting tonight. When things started to break, they were going to move fast. Ellery threw the paper down, disgusted by his own doubts.

Hell, yes, Reid. We're going to put this bastard away so you can keep making your trips to Gstaad every Christmas and going to Hong Kong on taxpayers' dollars without worrying about the plane blowing up. Channing's going to put her neck in the noose while you fuck your current secretary and your wife gets her hair done. I'm going to see she gets out in one piece. So she can go back to her life and I can go back to mine, and neither of us will think about each other once it's finished.

Ellery's heels bruised the concrete as he strode toward the lodge.

By day the indoor dining room had deep blue tablecloths and a menu that ranged from nouvelle California to pseudo Mexican. Ballieu had arrived first and rose to pull out a chair for Channing as she sat down. She'd changed into a green summer dress with one of her white jackets. The doctored film was on her. She had carried it ever since it had come into her possession. There was no way of predicting when Ballieu might decide to move.

"You found the tape?" Ballieu's solicitude sounded deliberately less than sincere. Again, as though they were playing a game, she thought.

"And took an opportunity to play it on a recorder the management kindly furnished," Channing said, matching his tone. "I'd hate to think we couldn't trust each other."

"Of course." He settled in across from her. She could feel them squaring off. "How charming to find you a woman of sentiment."

He started to pour her wine, but she asked the bar waiter already descending upon them for iced tea instead. She'd been drinking a lot of it here, which maybe explained why her nerves were jumpy. But better on edge than too relaxed, she rationalized.

Ballieu lounged back, his arm resting carelessly over the side of his chair.

"How long did you work for the man you're replacing?" he asked.

"Six years. Seven." Channing shrugged. "I'd known him all my life." There was always the possibility that Ballieu could check. If he did, she'd come up clean with this answer.

"And I never heard a breath about you? Amazing." His tone was mild but perhaps deceptive. His eyes were missing nothing. The care with which he noted the shape of her hair, the measure of her shoulders, each element in her made Channing want to draw back.

"I was a hidden asset." She forced her mouth into a teasing expression.

A waiter came. They placed their orders.

"You know"—Ballieu rocked his wine in its glass and continued to watch her—"there is something very intriguing about a woman willing to take the risks that you do. It hangs around her . . . like a musk."

The way he was looking at her made her queasy.

There was something blunt and repelling in it. An appetite.

Determination drove her, giving her a strange calm. Sitting here across from him was vindicating Yussuf in a way she couldn't quite explain.

"My work is safer than yours," she said, sidestepping his compliment.

"I've survived to an older age than you."

He smiled.

Before he could speak again, Channing saw the almost imperceptible quickening of his attention. He had noticed something over her right shoulder. Surely not Ellery. Surely Ellery wouldn't be that clumsy. Her pulse quickened. She turned as casually as any other dining companion might and saw a girl with long black hair sitting down at one of the tables. She'd been watching them avidly.

One of Ballieu's lady friends, jealous and keeping an eye on him? Channing wondered. She looked rather sulky. Whatever the situation, Ballieu didn't like it. He had frowned, but his face was smooth again.

Then their plates arrived, and with very little conversation they ate. It was all a charade, Channing thought. She was watching Ballieu. He was watching her. It took all her willpower just to keep from looking each time his pale hands poised and his knife sliced down at his food.

Am I a Stuart yet, Gramps? she thought silently, angrily. *It takes more audacity to sit here with him than to pass a silk through a rope under someone's nose.*

"So do we do business?" she asked when he'd

ordered coffee and she'd requested more tea. She was not as afraid of Ballieu as she'd been last night. She was holding her own.

"I never rush a decision," he said. "And we've plenty of time."

Damn. She was getting nothing out of him.

"Tell me about your operation," he said. "How the connection was made with Marinka, for example."

"We must have our secrets, just as you have yours."

Her answer seemed to amuse him.

"Ah, but we must trust each other, you said."

He was watching something over her shoulder. Some activity on the part of the girl with the black hair, no doubt. A moment later the waiter arrived to serve Ballieu's coffee and bring her a second serving of tea.

Channing frowned as she squeezed the lemon wedge from the side of the glass and pushed it down into the dark tea. Why had Ballieu wanted this meeting, and what should her next move be? She didn't dare force his hand.

Ballieu seemed to be looking at her now, but she had an unsettling feeling his eyes watched something else too. Had someone else come in behind her? Dry-mouthed, wondering how they would end this interview, she raised the cold glass of tea to her lips.

"Don't!"

Ballieu's hand shot out, knocking the glass from her hand. The glass hit the carpeted floor and cracked into two parts, its shaved ice scattering.

Drops of tea had splashed the arm of her jacket, spilling or bouncing back. Channing didn't know which.

She sat, scarcely able to breathe. The movement by Ballieu had been little more than a blur, almost as fast as she could change a coin. And in the instant her brain had registered his hand darting at her, she'd thought he held a gun.

"How clumsy of me," he said, passing her his napkin. "There was a crack in the glass. Very easy for germs to collect there. We wouldn't want you to fall sick."

She stared at him, trembling inside. *What had that move been about?* Had there been something in her glass? Had he been intending to poison her and at the last minute changed his mind?

"Perhaps you'll want to go and see to your jacket," he said. His eyes were hard.

Channing nodded. She rose and started out almost blindly. Max sat at a table near the door. His ailment must be improving. Face thoroughly ashen, he jerked a look at her and then back at Ballieu.

Ellery met her in the hall. He must have been inside the bar just off the dining room and seen it all, she realized. He caught her arm.

"What the hell happened? What was that all about?" He looked almost as tense as she was. The pressure of his fingers hurt.

"I don't know—but he scares me!"

The words rattled out in a gasp that sounded nothing like her own voice. Her doubled-up fist hit a button to summon an elevator.

She was furious hearing herself, furious hearing her own admission. For she knew fear was exactly the reaction Henri Ballieu was counting on. He had won this round.

Fourteen

As she opened the door to her room Ballieu slammed the insolent female who had been sent to help him into the wall. His fingers caught her throat as they might the loose skin on a kitten's neck.

"You stupid idiot!" he said, snarling.

Her eyes were filled with rage, not submission. She had come to her room directly from the restaurant, knowing he would follow. She caught his wrist in a soldier's grip. Her defiance hissed out in spite of his hold on her.

"You ruined it—she would be dead!"

She twisted, bringing her shoulder up against him and almost breaking free. Once more Ballieu slammed her against the wall.

"She'd be dead when we might need her! If anything goes wrong—if the men try to stop us—don't you realize her value as a pawn? What did you put in her tea when you stopped the waiter? Those splinters of glass you were so eager to try?"

"Yes! And they'll soon be carting those Zionist brats off with belly pains too! No one would have suspected. I planned very well!"

Ballieu shook his head with fury. He'd discarded his watch behind a picture frame as he got off the elevator to her floor and could speak freely.

"You've done nothing well!"

He wanted to kill her. But you didn't kill your own kind. Not unless they deserved it. His breath was coming in short gasps as he thought how she'd nearly destroyed all their chances when they were within a single day of putting their hands on the film. With her hotheadedness she could have come between him and the successful completion of this assignment. If she'd killed the Stuart woman, the other Americans would have been left no choice but to retaliate. He spun his young helper around and struck the side of her face.

"Fool!" he repeated. "Daughter of dogs!"

He started to tell her he'd see she never again received a job more important than polishing boots. Then, with the cold reason that had always given him mastery, he realized he still needed her. Tonight, especially. Ballieu changed tactics.

"You're very talented, Khadija." His voice had become detached. Almost patient. That of teacher to student. "You could be quite valuable someday. Why do you not follow orders?"

Her whole face sneered at him.

"You think you can report me for this, don't you, Ballieu? But I'll report how you've lost your nerve. I'll report how there's something wrong with your belly!"

By the time he felt her shifting, her foot drove in. Ballieu felt an explosion of white, blinding pain. She sprang free of his momentarily loosened fingers. He lunged, and she fell backward, taking him with her and flipping him over her. He rolled expertly, completing the somersault to land on his feet.

Already she was crouched to receive his attack.

They circled each other. Her hands were held open and loose, silent weapons that would not be heard outside this room with its air-conditioning and padded carpeting.

"What's wrong, Ballieu? Can't you kill a woman?" Her words taunted him. "Is that why you sit down with her, talk with her, knowing any instant that she could betray you? Or are you sniffing after her the way you did that whore you hired?"

Ballieu felt each muscle and nerve in his body tuning itself. The precision needed to kill or maim was flowing through him.

"She's unimportant," he said. Because he needed this unstable female who thought to challenge him, and he would let her live. But he was closing in. "Untrained. It's the man with her who controls her. He tells her what to do. She'll be nothing without him. They'll allow us one kill if they think they can learn who the seller is. Not two. It would leave too bitter a taste in their mouths. Understand what I say."

He wondered fleetingly why there was such a flush of triumph on Khadija's cheeks and why her eyes directed such hatred toward him.

Khadija spit.

"Excuses! You'll never get that film. You've gotten yourself in a hole and will never get out! You'll accomplish nothing!"

He measured the distance. He couldn't strike her again; it would show. He had to leave her unblemished so she could mingle unnoticed with the hotel's guests. They continued to circle. His movement, when it came, was like lightning, cutting the edge of his hand up under her jaw, bringing the toe of his shoe hard into the sensitive spot between her legs.

Ballieu had the satisfaction of hearing her whine in pain. Immediately he pinned her against the hard surface of the desk. It had entered his mind, the display of dominance a woman like this would find most bitter—the kind most likely to teach her her place. His hand caught at her skirt and thrust it up.

One side of her face was bleeding in spite of his efforts to leave no signs. He'd thought to see fear. Instead there was only her all-consuming rage. With black hair sprawled around her, choking against the hand that pressed down on her throat, she laughed wildly.

"Go ahead, Ballieu. Rape your own daughter. Or don't you even remember Saleha Adawi?"

He wavered, stunned. It was a brilliant tactic.

But no. She wasn't lying. With shock he recalled at last where he'd seen eyes like hers.

"She thought you were a god," the girl continued. "Everyone thought you were a god. I got so sick of hearing it, I decided to see for myself!"

Unwittingly he had released the pressure on her throat. Now, though he did not press, he doubled his caution.

"So what?" he said coldly. "Men and women come together, they part."

But her words had dazed him.

He thought of Saleha Adawi. A very attractive woman. A long time ago. It suddenly seemed he could feel his life slipping from him, second by second, joining other things that were past. His anger increased as he realized his mind had wandered.

"You discredit your brothers and sisters, taking this assignment out of personal selfishness," he said. "The individual counts for nothing in our cause—only the cause itself. You're not fit to belong to your organization!"

Beneath her sullenness she began to look frightened. Ballieu felt a quiver pass through him. Instinct told him to complete his act of violence, to break her once and for all, yet he was repelled by the news she'd flung in his face. A thought cast its shadow over his mind. Did he really want to satisfy himself with the American woman as this one suggested?

Roughly he pushed himself free and turned, straightening his collar.

"Do exactly as you're told from here on out," he warned, "or I'll kill you myself."

She twisted onto her side, her voice calling harshly after him as he reached the door.

"I am your surprise against them, Ballieu. You need me."

Ballieu smiled to himself. Her voice lacked conviction.

The episode in the restaurant was fading because she willed it to fade. Channing sat in a chair in her room with her feet up and fingertips pressed lightly to her forehead. Serafin sprawled on her bed. The draperies were drawn against the afternoon sun. Their surroundings were dusky. On the floor between them a small tape recorder filled the room, and their thoughts, with Yussuf's voice.

". . . and the king of hearts is upside down."

Channing still felt shaky, her mind filled with an image of flying glass rather than the words she was hearing. Had there been something in her drink? Had Ballieu intended to kill her and then changed his mind for some reason? Or had it been some sort of test?

Worse than the unanswered questions, she kept rechurning the knowledge that Ellery had witnessed her lapse in composure. He'd have two reasons now to doubt her ability to carry out the job entrusted to her: today's reaction after Ballieu swept the glass away; and yesterday's snag with the practice film.

She listened to Yussuf's instructions trail off for a third time, as disturbing now as they had been when she'd first listened. Disturbing because they sounded so innocent and summoned such recollections of good times shared, she thought, rubbing her forehead. Disturbing because they *were* so innocent—a cherished magic trick. Whether Yussuf had felt some premonition that he was in over his head, or whether he'd planned to disappear, he'd wanted to leave her this legacy.

There was only the scratch of the tape winding toward its end to break the silence.

"Maybe if we played it backwards or something," ventured Serafin. There was a waver in his voice.

"No." Channing scooted down in her chair and looked toward the ceiling, its actual margins softened and obscured by the dimness. "It's what he said it was. His special trick, which he invented and no one has ever figured out. That's all."

Along with sadness she felt relief. Serafin would start to heal now. He would see Yussuf had been something more than the deceiver painted for them by recent events. He would see that he himself hadn't been just some sort of dupe.

"Part of him was really good, then?"

"Yes," she said softly.

A lie? Channing wasn't sure. She didn't know what to think anymore, didn't know how you measured things.

She recalled what she'd said to Ellery that morning. In the course of their lives everyone did some variety of sleight of hand. The thought depressed her now. Yussuf had hidden what he was—under glitter, under laughter. He'd deceived people who had admired him; he'd betrayed an entire profession.

The tape snapped off. She roused herself for Serafin's sake.

"Part of Yussuf was really good," she reiterated. "The part that was your friend. The part that was my friend. I think he probably would have taken you with him the way he promised—just as he left me this tape."

She needed to affirm it for the boy, to help him accept what had happened.

Or did she need the affirmation herself?

She was thirty-two years old and felt every day of it just now, she realized, closing her eyes and pressing them. The backs of her arms ached from their hours of unaccustomed practice. Her confidence in her own ability ebbed and flowed, then ebbed again. She was disgusted with herself for letting Ballieu rattle her.

Maybe Ellery had been right to consider her a liability. Yet when she'd been a child, performing under Gramps's proud tutelage, she'd occasionally blown a sleight or a trick she'd thought perfected. She'd learned you didn't just quit. You didn't crawl into a hole. You studied what had gone wrong and you worked harder. You went on.

"Channing?"

In the dimness of the room she could hear Serafin move closer. She opened her eyes and met the bright, childlike anger in his.

"The man you're after is the one who killed Yussuf, isn't he? I want you to get him, Channing!"

"I want that too," she said, and meant it.

Henri Ballieu had robbed both of them of Yussuf in a way that merely killing him could never have done. She might be older than Serafin, but she shared his feeling.

Reaching out to turn on a light, she brought a piece of film to her fingertips and gave it a practice snap. She was worried. The card shaver hadn't arrived. Rundell should have found it and had it on its way to her this morning. She'd tried calling him several times but had gotten no answer. There was nothing for her to do except wait—and practice.

Matching action to thought, she rose and walked toward the draperied window. The change in position gave all the privacy she required. Her hand moved almost automatically, performing the substitution. She'd accomplished it flawlessly hundreds of times since yesterday's snag. It had to have been a thread in the jacket she'd worn. Or the edge of the film.

"Have we been resting long enough to go to the pool again?" Serafin asked.

She shook her head.

"We're supposed to stay in the room until three o'clock. Ellery said."

Either he wanted a break from baby-sitting, she thought, or he had something else to do.

It was hot in the back of the van, and Oliver Lemming sounded tenser and more irritable than usual.

"There are houses up in the hills in that direction," he snapped, gesturing. "Not lots, but maybe thirty or so. And a town ten miles away, even if it's not much. This safe the film's supposedly in could be anywhere—if it's all not a lot of baloney. What do you think, Bill? I can get some sort of general search warrant so you can go poking. I thought you'd studied law!"

They glared at each other. Ellery blotted sweat from his chin. The van they were meeting in was painted with the name of a commercial linen service, and Oliver wore the coveralls of a delivery man. No question he rolled up his sleeves and worked with his troops when he deemed it necessary. Whereas other field supervisors were content to run an operation from a command post, Oliver left nothing to chance. He assessed the territory. He assessed his people. He checked in once a day to sift through the nuances that could be missed by relying on radio contact. The only thing he wasn't doing was giving them a hell of a lot of help, thought Ellery.

His resentment spilled out in words.

"For chrissake, Oliver! You can't get a warrant. You can't get us more help. You haven't even gotten us an ID on those photographs—"

Oliver exploded, his silver brows drawing together. "What the hell's the matter with you? We only got the frigging photographs four hours ago! You're sounding like a mother hen. Maybe it was a mistake to put you with a woman."

"Yeah. Maybe it was."

Their eyes locked.

Ellery felt the heat beating in through the roof of the van. Oliver looked away first and started to pace as well as he could in the cramped space.

"Sorry," he said abruptly. "You know as well as I do how things work."

Ellery nodded. What Oliver had said about trying to locate the film was reasonable. They both knew it. He was being too protective of Channing. They both knew that too.

Still, if they put their minds to it, the alternative he was suggesting was surely feasible.

"She's nervous." He pressed his argument, anyway, not mentioning Channing's name. He wondered why that was. "If we could find where they've stashed the film, we could switch it ourselves. No risks involved."

"And miss who's selling the film." Oliver brought his sharp scrutiny to bear on Ellery. "How do you rate her? Apart from nervous."

Ellery tightened his jaw. He'd always respected Oliver, and every decision made depended on candor between them.

"Good. She's damned good. She's got a knack for playing off people and situations that's plain uncanny—the entertainer in her, I guess. Ballieu threw her a real curve when he asked her about the timing device, but she held her own.

"You were right. She's smart. And she doesn't panic. But yesterday she muffed the film once. What if that happens when it's for real?"

Oliver grunted.

"She practicing?"

"From what I've seen of her, I'd guess that's all she's doing. She could be doing it under my nose, for all I know."

He thought about how she'd pulled that button off his shirt and then reattached it.

"Then we take our chances," the older man said. "One slip in a thousand's pretty good odds." He looked at his watch, a hint that they ought to wrap this meeting up. "If you get a fix on the film tonight, I'll get a warrant," he conceded. "Be careful tailing Ballieu."

Ellery nodded stiffly. He'd gone into situations without a backup before. It was part of the game. Things weren't always perfect.

He reached for the door and felt Oliver's hand on his shoulder.

"I've had some second thoughts about this plan myself," said Oliver. "Every time I send people on an assignment I know could turn nasty, I have a few. Watch out for yourself, Bill. And watch out for her."

* * *

Khadija fingered the cut on her face and then the sack of plastic explosive hidden beneath stacks of underwear. She was glad she hadn't disposed of the plastique when Ballieu told her to. She was glad she hadn't obeyed him. Her head hurt from its pounding against the wall. Ballieu thought he had broken her. He hadn't.

The arrogant old man had been entirely unmoved by her revelation. The news of their relationship hadn't shaken him. It hadn't pushed him to anger; or to the denial she'd been eager to refute; or to the surprised, then patronizing, acknowledgment of her which she could have scorned. It simply hadn't mattered to him. He hadn't even asked about her mother.

Pig.

Lighting a long, dark cigarette, she sucked its strength in. Another breath and she irritably ground out the burning end against a table. She let the idea that had started to come dance through her mind. She dressed it in details, then came back to present resentments.

They could be on their way already. She could have opened the vault and they could have stolen a car and gone across the Mexican border. But Ballieu waited.

He didn't believe in her competence, she thought angrily. Or he couldn't acknowledge it. That was how it happened when a man got old. He held jealously to his power. It was why she didn't dare act entirely on her own. Ballieu would discredit her.

But surely she would be applauded if she accomplished more than smuggling out the piece of film. With jerky motions Khadija again lit the end of the cigarette. She had been trained not to waste. It seemed such a waste not to use the sack of explosive in the drawer by her elbow.

In her own group she was a leader. There were many, in other groups as well as her own, who said she was as good as Ballieu himself had been at her age. She was ready to move into the sort of job that Ballieu performed. But Ballieu wasn't giving her a chance to prove herself.

Like needles of blowing sand, a sense of powerlessness stung at her. She must do as instructed tonight. Still, she would see her name was not disgraced. While Ballieu played his waiting game she would show some initiative.

After washing her face she combed her hair carefully over the small cut that was coming to be a reminder of her personal mission. She glossed her lips and sprayed herself with cologne. Now she was ready to go downstairs.

It should not take long to determine where, in this place clogged with unobservant vacationers, the most Americans could be found at any one time, she thought. It should not take long to discover where her sack of explosive could do the most damage.

Fifteen

"Here're the ID reports on those photographs you sent in," said Walker, tossing them at Ellery. "Came in while Max was in the can. Good thing I was here."

"Jesus. Do I have to listen to this for the rest of my life?" objected Max. He was hooked to the headset.

Ballieu had just returned to his room, presumably to dress for dinner, so Walker was unexpectedly free to touch base with the rest of them. They'd have a full house when Channing arrived.

Ellery scanned the sheets in front of him. A student, a dance instructor, and a wealthy widow. Not a scrap on any of them. A dead end. He looked up to see Walker pouring a shot of cold coffee and Max watching the back of the ID sheets with the face of one who'd already seen their contents.

"Can't always count on hunches, Billy," he said with a shrug. "We knew it was a long shot. Ballieu's always worked alone."

Dropping the papers back on the desk, Ellery nodded. His mind wouldn't let it go.

There had to be some purpose behind Ballieu's socializing. A man who pulled off the sort of things Ballieu had simply didn't enjoy himself. Not on the job, anyway.

It occurred to Ellery that maybe he was grasping

at straws, so determined to tip the odds in their favor that he was deceiving himself. What did he know about a man like Ballieu? Sure, he could name the man's habits and ways of operating, but maybe he'd fallen into the trap of otherwise thinking of people like Ballieu stereotypically—no feelings apart from fanaticism, no vices.

He heard the door opening. That would be Channing. She came in twiddling a coin through half closed fingers. Max leaned closer, dropping his voice.

"What do you think about our lady? She looked pretty shaken up over what Ballieu pulled in the restaurant."

"Yeah, well, you didn't look so good yourself," Ellery shot back.

Max grinned.

"Lunch in the service of my country set my recovery back by a good couple hours. I was being serious, Billy."

Ellery watched the woman they were talking about. This was the second time today someone had asked him to evaluate her. It struck him that maybe that was how life was for women: always being evaluated, either on looks if they were being judged as bed or marriage fodder, or because of some unvoiced belief that they weren't quite equal to men if they were being eyed for the workplace.

"She'll do," he answered.

He felt a little guilty understating it but figured anything else would be wasted on Max. Max stirred his elegant form.

"Hey, Channing. Special stock, just for you."

Reaching over, he opened a can of V-8. He poured the contents over ice and held it toward her. She looked surprised.

"Thanks," she said, joining them.

"She brought me a present," said Walker. Sourly he displayed the expensive-looking cigar in his hand. "The question is, will it blow up when I smoke it?"

"Try it," urged Max.

"So what do we do now? Synchronize watches or what?"

Channing sounded nettled—or maybe hurt—by Walker's suspicion, Ellery noted.

"Just checking for loose ends before we head into the evening," said Max.

Ellery saw her flinch. She'd theorized that her slip with the film had been the fault of a loose thread, and this was reminding her of it.

"Any more trouble with that new trick you're trying?" he asked.

Her eyes shot to his. She'd understood. She knew he was asking about her practice, but she'd misinterpreted his meaning.

"Not a bit."

Her shoulders were rigid.

Annoyed with her as well as with himself, Ellery took her elbow. He turned her away from the others.

"Look, I wasn't riding you," he said.

She tried to withdraw. He didn't let her.

"You have a right to. You're the one who'll be on the spot if I screw up," she said.

"We'll both be on the spot," he said, correcting her grimly.

He let her go. It bothered him that he liked touching her.

She glanced back at the others, then plunged her hands into her pockets.

"You're still going out by yourself tonight?"

Ellery nodded.

She looked at him a long moment, and he knew she wanted to argue. Instead she shrugged.

"Then there's not much point in my sticking around here, is there? Thanks for the juice, Max," she called, heading toward the door.

It slammed behind her, shaking the whole wall. Walker looked up questioningly from his still unlighted cigar. Ellery felt an urge to drag her back and chew her out about making a scene, but he felt a contradictory urge to kick himself.

"Lovers' quarrel?" asked Max with a grin.

"You're worried about Ellery, huh?" asked Serafin, making swishing moves with a wand Channing had given him.

He didn't have any technique as yet, but he showed a great flair for showmanship, Channing thought. She applied a stroke of eyeliner and methodically blurred its edges. Their dressing room was cramped and felt stuffy tonight.

"Why should I worry about Ellery?"

She stole a look at Serafin, a little annoyed, as she was from time to time, that he somehow knew more about what was going on than he should. About the plans laid to keep track of Ballieu's movements tonight, for instance. His eyes blinked back at her as if they were an owl's. Or camera lenses. He shrugged, apparently dismissing the subject.

Channing busied herself with the rest of her makeup. The fact was, she had been thinking of Ellery. It made her uneasy that he was going out alone tonight. It incensed her she still was deemed unsuitable to help somewhere along the line. She wondered if Ballieu had possibly seen through her act about Yussuf, and if he'd put something in her glass at noon. She wondered if she'd ever drink iced tea again.

"He likes you," said Serafin, still on the subject of Ellery.

"That's nice." She whisked away the towel at her neck to reveal the long unused costume she'd dragged out of mothballs for this engagement. The jacket was shimmering gold, banded with black on the cuffs and lapels to match the high-necked blouse she wore beneath. The flowing black pants looked vaguely Oriental.

"Aw, come on. You don't want to wind up an old maid, do you?" Serafin pressed.

"That," said Channing, wiping her palms with a towel and putting it carefully aside, "is an archaic term."

"But—"

"Dammit, Serafin! Let me alone, will you?"

The abruptness of her temper made her feel guilty. Maybe there were things she didn't want to face. Maybe she'd gotten careless and let herself do what she'd never meant to do again—start to care. About a man who took unnecessary risks out of pure stubbornness, who was going out with an injured shoulder.

"Ellery's going to go his way when this is finished, and I'll go mine," she said. She checked her pockets as she'd watched Yussuf checking his the night she'd slipped in on him. "I don't know why I keep talking to you as if you're an adult."

Serafin grinned.

A knock sounded at the dressing room door. Channing turned with a wave of uneasiness.

"Everything okay this evening?" asked Wilbur, beaming in at her when she answered.

The light from the hall reflected off his balding head. An armload of fragrant red roses engulfed her in sweetness from another world as he passed them to her.

"I—uh—thought you might like these. I may get a chance to see your act tonight. If there's not a crisis."

Aware of movement behind her, Channing's peripheral vision tuned in to the end of Serafin's thumb-and-forefinger "okay" sign.

"I'll look for you in the audience," she said, and thanked him, closing the door. She turned to Serafin with a narrow look. "What was that all about?"

"I told him a bunch of roses would probably get him in good with you." Serafin squirmed a little in the face of her silence. "Aw, come on, Channing. He's had a bad day. Some kids who checked out complained of stomachaches when they got home, so the health department's been here inspecting the kitchen. I had to do something for him for letting me hang around so much. And it's for a good cause."

For a good cause. Was that how Ellery rationalized taking risks? There was a job to do, and no one else to do it, and so he would? She almost laughed at the irony. It sounded like Tony.

Holding the roses carefully out from her sleeves, she marched across the room and laid them on her dressing table. She wiped her hands again. A knot that she thought must be disgust or indignation had lodged in her chest. In the paper she'd seen that photograph of the man she realized must be Ellery's brother, bathed in publicity while Ellery was risking his life—alone—tonight.

She recalled what Ellery had let slip when he'd shown her his grandfather's watch. That was what drove him—he had ghosts to slay. She understood it even as she hated it. She, too, had something to prove. To Gramps.

Twenty minutes later she and Serafin went onstage. Henri Ballieu sat waiting, in the second row.

Ballieu had vomited blood in the lavatory before he came to dinner. It didn't concern him. Victory was too close now. Every moment was bringing it nearer, and everything was planned. He had eaten a hearty dinner to restore his strength. Shish kebab on rice pilaf. A plate of cheeses. Fruit. He could still taste the sweetness of melon dripping across his tongue. He had ordered brandy and sat toying with the snifter without sipping it.

The revelation of the girl who was the product of his nights with Saleha Adawi meant nothing to him.

He felt no emotion at all at the link between them. She was a flawed piece of merchandise whose defects, like those of a rifle whose scope was off, must be taken into account. He could predict her now and had proved his superiority. She would do well enough in the small chores left to her. The first show of the evening ended with the last song of a particularly uninteresting singer, and Ballieu applauded.

It had been very easy to watch the magic act. There was something fascinating about the Stuart woman, particularly now that he knew what she was. A dark elusiveness like the shadow of fire seemed to cling to her. As though she might conjure a scarf and snap her fingers under the nose of death itself, Ballieu thought with admiration. The way in which her entire being challenged his excited him. A pity they would not have more time.

Ballieu looked at his watch. Khadija, who was sitting somewhere in the back of the room, would leave now. As soon as the magic act began a second time, he would leave too. His contact had assured him that the U.S. agents would all be occupied—two of them staying upstairs, one following him to the place of rendezvous, and the Stuart woman in front of her audience. His strategy was simple, yet effective.

When the lights dimmed for the second show, Ballieu reached casually under his watchband and removed the bug. When the magician, in her glittering costume, appeared again, he rose and dropped the listening device in a potted plant, then left the room.

The bug would continue to broadcast sounds of

the show in progress. Whoever was listening upstairs would find nothing amiss. The man who followed him probably had no way of monitoring the listening device but would follow in any case, perhaps even hopeful of being led to the film itself.

As Ballieu's car turned out of the entrance to the parking lot, his check of the rearview mirror picked up another car pulling out. It showed no lights. Ballieu grunted his satisfaction.

Everything was in readiness. The snares were ready to spring. He was pleased he'd had the foresight to order the two well-built rifles with infrared scopes. He was about to make his escape with the film a great deal easier.

Sixteen

Channing entered the dressing room, dropped the nesting silver boxes from the last number in her act, and fanned the lapels of her hot jacket. She'd seen Ballieu leave—had been waiting subconsciously for him to make the move—and her uneasiness was mounting. His timing had been too careful, waiting till she'd come onstage. She threw down a handful of coins that had been in her pocket. Damn.

She wasn't sure if it was logic or some gut feeling that kept pushing at her. But she was sure she couldn't let Ellery take a chance he didn't have to take. Decision made, she spun and almost collided with Serafin. His arms were laden with a few of her more valuable props. His face went motionless with speculation.

"Serafin—"

"—go stick with Wilbur. I know." He was at her heels as she hit the hall. He hurried to keep pace with her. "Sure you don't need me with you?"

His voice held a thread of worry. Berating herself that she'd let her anxiety show, Channing shook her head.

"I don't expect to be too long. I'll just feel better—"

"—if I'm not alone. I know. Hey, Wilbur!" he called in the same breath. They had reached the lobby. The assistant manager was checking something at the desk.

"Is there a rock shaped like a cat somewhere around here?" Channing cut in as Wilbur started to speak.

"Oh, you must mean Puma Rock. Out that way, about twenty minutes from here. Nice place to picnic when it's not too hot. Say, would you like to—"

"How do you get there?"

Poor Wilbur looked crestfallen.

"It's that dead-end road off the main drag. Leads right to it. But you're not going *now*—"

"No, just out for a breath of air," said Channing, already at the door. "See you later, Serafin."

She took two more almost normal steps before breaking into a run toward her jeep. A spare key was fastened under the front bumper, held in place by a catch it would take a Stuart's trained hand to unfasten. Channing felt a seam at her shoulder rip as she stooped for the key. A moment later she was behind the wheel, spinning out toward the main road.

The landscape she passed looked nothing like it had in daytime. A few twisted trees reached up out of desolate barenness. Rock ledges carved by erosion called to mind a dead and abandoned planet. Even the glitter of stars through the clear air didn't soften the sense of waste everywhere as Channing shot by.

Her foot was too hard on the accelerator. She knew it and thanked whatever force guided human affairs that she met no other traffic. Ghosts seemed to be in the jeep with her. The one that had been Tony and the one that could be Ellery. As different as night and day, she thought: the one who was dead no matter what she did; and the one who was part of the here and now.

She missed the ruts leading off to the right until she had passed them. Hitting her brakes, she backed up, swung off onto the dead end, and killed her lights. There was no hope of speed now. She crept along over rough terrain, glad for her sturdy jeep. The track she was following twisted steeply up, and so far there was nothing around that resembled a cat—or a puma. In the darkness ahead, broken here and there by scrubby growth or a twisted tree, she could barely make out the first shapes of a boulder field.

Suddenly her foot reached for the brake. She could see the outline of a car to the side of the road. Impossible to tell the color, or even the shape, but she thought it must be Ellery's to be this far back.

What if she'd endangered him by coming here? The thought entered her mind for the first time. What if her arrival called attention to him or disrupted whatever meeting was taking place?

Rundell would have been the first to point out the dangers of her impulsiveness, she thought bitterly. Maybe this was a perfect example of why Ellery had been leery of working with her. As she hesitated, hand hovering over the gearshift, torn between instinct and common sense, the darkness ahead split open with the ominous cracks of a shooting gallery.

* * *

Ellery hit the ground and rolled as a dead tree exploded just over his head. One of the particles lodged in his eye. He rolled again, instinctively.

Night scopes, he thought as another volley of shots ricocheted off the rock that was sheltering him. They'd have to be using them to come this close to hitting him. The shots were coming from two directions. He'd walked into a trap.

He crawled on his belly, zigzagging, jerking back, and rolling again as the shots tried to track him. His only hope was to find a rock with a larger overhang or to make his way out, the latter being very unlikely. He'd left the car too far away, figuring Ballieu and whomever he was meeting would be here already and parked closer in. Blinking the speck of wood from his watering eye, he cursed his own failure of judgment.

How the hell had they known he was there? He wore rubber-soled running shoes. He'd moved without making a sound. They had to be watching for him. . . .

A shot whanged into the rock above him. No time for thinking. He slithered and twisted, the pistol in his right hand useless.

He hit the side of the boulder he'd been aiming for and found its contour smooth to the ground, useless as shelter. If he died here, what would they tell his mother and Reid? That he'd been some low-level State Department researcher? The truth? No matter. Either way he'd go out in his family's eyes with the same reputation he'd always had—a failure.

Ellery gritted his teeth. He wasn't going to fail. He gathered his muscles for action and leapt toward the shape of a tree.

A half instant later his overtaxed brain gave form to a sound he'd heard but hadn't recognized, a car engine bearing toward him. He saw it just as a volley of shots from above turned in its direction, shattering what sounded like a headlight. It swerved as if one of the tires were hit, but then he realized that the swerving was deliberate. It was coming purposely but erratically into the mouth of the dead end. The fire from above divided between him and the new target.

The passenger's door on the jeep flew open, and it skidded around in a half circle, almost out of control.

"Ellery!" a voice from inside called sharply.

"Jesus Christ!" he said under his breath.

Channing was following the line of the shots to locate him. She swooped again, and her open door gave him partial cover.

"Here!" he called, gathering himself for the sprint across open ground.

Bullets shattered the glass in the door as he caught hold of it. Channing peeled out almost before he heaved himself in by the back of the seat. He was nearly thrown on top of her. She veered adroitly to elude the rain of shots that hit her right fender.

"You always drive like a drunken bat?" He panted, bracing himself.

"You always take dumb-ass chances?" she shouted back as her wrists whipped the wheel.

But she grinned, her eyes never leaving the road, and Ellery, ducking a shot, knew she was aware he had returned the grin. The night, which thirty seconds ago he'd thought would be his last, seemed suddenly fine.

"Why'd you do it?" he asked as another shot whizzed by. They both flinched.

She concentrated on driving. The gears grated as she tried for a higher speed to get them away from the boulders.

"I've never liked lousy odds."

Ellery found himself letting in all the sensations he'd locked out. Admiration for the sense of right and wrong that drove her. Anticipation of their arguments. Attraction to the set of her mouth and the speed of her mind. The question of whether in a lifetime anyone could figure her out, and whether she'd let anyone get close enough to try.

They were almost out of range of the rifles now, but a final bullet cracked through the jeep. Channing's head jerked sideways, hitting the driver's window. She slumped, her hands dropping from the wheel.

Ellery grabbed to recover it, wrestling the vehicle a short distance down the rough trail, out of reach of the powerful rifles. He stopped, the most mind-numbing fear he'd ever known in his life pounding through him. The woman who had joked beside him a moment before was motionless, her mesmerizing energy snuffed out. Her hair had escaped the elaborate arrangement she wore onstage. It tangled about her.

Telling himself he shouldn't waste this time, that

he should just get the hell back to report what had happened, he touched her chin.

"Channing?"

His voice was rough. His tongue felt swollen. A sense of something lost that might have been his if he'd reached for it glimmered and went out in front of him as he turned her head.

His fingers found the wetness before he saw it. Blood was trickling down from her left temple.

Seventeen

"Damn."

Her voice, thick with irritation, reassured him just as Ellery pushed back her hair. She'd knocked herself out when her head hit the window. The blood was from a cut—broken glass, maybe.

"You okay?"

He leaned back as she raised a hand to the side of her forehead. He saw her wince. Still seeming a little groggy, she glared at him, then pushed herself erect.

"No. I'll have a lump the size of an egg on my forehead tomorrow. And half the routines I'm using are just the way Gramps did them—not mine at all!"

Ellery rested his shoulders against the seat, chuckling with relief at the grit that fueled her. The sound of her swearing had been like music. That mumbo jumbo about her routine showed she was still disoriented. He'd bet it also betrayed a professional ego she'd like to deny she had.

"Come on. If we don't get moving, Ballieu's guards could catch up with us again," he said. "Switch places with me." Reaching out, he lifted her across his lap, sliding under her.

They seemed to stall midway through the transfer, pressed face-to-face by the cramped confines of the jeep's interior. Ellery could feel the warmth of her waist beneath his hands. He could feel her breathing. The change in its rhythm told him she wanted him as much as he suddenly wanted her. Or maybe it wasn't so suddenly, after all. It had been building for days—since he met her.

One move. That was all it would take from either of them. Only there wasn't time.

With an effort of will equal to any he'd ever made in his life, Ellery eased her into the passenger seat and put the jeep into gear. It slipped down the dirt road and onto pavement. He switched on its lights.

"You seem to have a headlight gone," he said to break the tension.

"Yes. And a few scratches here and there. Think they'll give me a good price on trade-in?"

Her voice sounded strained.

There was no sign of a car behind them. When he'd been on foot, he'd passed Ballieu's, parked farther in than where he'd left his, but Ballieu and whoever had been with him out there weren't giving chase. The first ugly thoughts about what had happened back in those boulders started to swarm through Ellery's mind.

Beside him, Channing had lapsed into silence. Not because of what had almost happened between them a few minutes earlier, Ellery thought. She seemed to have put that aside as completely as he had. When he glanced to make sure she hadn't passed out again from the bump to her head, he saw she was frowning. A coin danced back and forth across the back of her closed hand, a restless, shimmering waterfall of motion.

"Those weren't guards back there," she said.

He had turned his attention back to the road. Now he shot a sharper look at her. Her eyes were brooding.

"There's nothing to guard," she said, turning to evaluate his reaction. "No building—no place for a safe unless it's built into rock. That was a setup."

Reluctantly Ellery nodded.

"Ballieu let us overhear those phone calls deliberately, so we'd spread ourselves thin. He must have found the bug. Your cover's blown."

"I'll convince him I'm working my own game."

"No. I want you and Serafin to clear out tonight."

"It wasn't me he was after, or he wouldn't have scheduled his shooting party so close to the end of my act!"

The vehemence suddenly present in her words made him dread the turn the conversation was going to take. She drew breath carefully.

"Damn it, Ellery, hasn't it occurred to you there's another way Ballieu could have learned about the bug?"

They were nearing the turnoff to Palacio Sol. Ellery slowed the jeep and eased it toward the entrance, his face averted.

They seemed to think alike sometimes. He'd started to realize it in these few days they'd spent together. She was rational and intelligent, and what she was suggesting confirmed the suspicions that were starting to bite at him.

"It *has* occurred to you, hasn't it?" she said more softly.

"That someone could have told Ballieu what was in his watch? Somebody we thought was on our side?" Ellery coasted the battered vehicle into a parking place as out-of-the-way as he could find and silenced the engine. "Yeah. It's occurred to me."

The possibility was sucking at him like an undertow, pulling everything he believed in, everything he'd worked for out from under him. He fought a drowning feeling, held afloat only by his own anger. Somebody he'd trusted could be as crooked as Yussuf had been. Somebody he and Channing thought was helping might be willing to kill them.

And suddenly he knew this assignment had narrowed down to just the two of them. Him and Channing. He and the woman he'd scorned as an amateur but had come to admire. She was his partner now, the only one he could trust. It had nothing to do with his attraction to her as a woman—he'd be a fool to base judgment on that. It had to do with the fact she'd saved his tail tonight, and with what she was saying now, with her directness. They sat amid shards of glass, neither of them moving.

"It sure as hell would explain a lot of things," he acknowledged. "How Ballieu knew to tear out the first bugs we planted. Why that other room Yussuf reserved is unoccupied. How the film disappeared in the first place. It all falls into place if the seller is one of us."

He realized she might not know what he was talking about. The film had disappeared a while ago, back when Sam was alive. With a grimace he backtracked.

"We were all in Washington when it happened. Me. Sam. Oliver. Max and Walker. Lots of other people—all in to debrief a big case."

Frowning, he looked back in time. Patterns that hadn't been apparent started to emerge.

"We assumed that whoever initially stole the film did it by accident. That they thought the people moving it were moving money. Maybe we've been wrong from the first. Maybe whoever killed those couriers knew exactly what he was getting."

Channing leaned against the frame of the shattered window behind her.

"The people at your meeting knew when the film was moving?"

"Not the time, especially. Just that it would move and that it would be that day. It wasn't a big thing—had nothing to do with us—just a comment one of the bigwigs made in passing. I guess the fact that the theft occurred practically under our noses made us all a little extra indignant."

He reached for the handle of the door beside him and shoved it to release the anger building inside him.

"Some of us, anyway," he said correcting himself.

Someone he'd worked with was a traitor. And a killer.

They met in front of the jeep and fell into step together.

"Ellery?" Her voice slipped into huskiness. As she looked up, he saw she had dirt and dried blood on the side of her face. "I'm sorry."

"Yeah. Me too," he said. "I thought I was working for a high-class outfit."

He took her arm. It felt right. They walked through the night together.

Ellery was aware of silence building until at last he spoke what was on his mind.

"It'd be risky, trying to make Ballieu and whoever else we're up against think you're flimflamming us," he said.

He didn't know how he could even consider it, except that, like taking her arm, it seemed right.

"It's my world too," she said lightly. "I move around in it more than most people. You're not going to tell me I don't have to pay my dues because I'm a female, are you?"

Ellery didn't answer.

They could abort the whole mission, go to Oliver with their suspicions, and, because the odds were too clearly against Channing's switch, pull out. It would mean instant safety for the two of them, and they could still nab Ballieu—maybe. Not a total loss. But if they were right about a traitor on their team, not playing things through could give that individual a chance to vanish back into the woodwork. He could stay with the department for years, impossible to smoke out and committing God knows what acts of treason in the years to come.

Treason. Ellery's mind replayed the word. It was something out of law texts, not part of day-to-day life. Until now.

They were nearing a door to the lodge. He looked at Channing. If State had a crooked agent, catching him was just as important as switching the film. Maybe more so. She understood that.

The hell of it was, he couldn't think of anyone else he'd feel even halfway comfortable asking for help.

He wanted to protect her, yet to do so would deny some vital part of her.

"Better clean up," he said, stopping to survey her. "I'd rather give you credit for your rescue efforts, but if no one knows who bailed me out, you'll stand a better chance of peddling your story."

"You want me to go in as if I've been strolling around the grounds or something?"

"Right. I'll use another door and go up to the listening post. Meet me there and we'll play it the same."

One sleeve of her gold jacket had split loose from the shoulder seam to hang raggedly. She took the jacket off and swung it over her shoulder.

"Have a comb?" She began to remove the few pins left straggling from her hair.

"Do I look like Max?" He grinned. "Never carry one."

Licking the inside of his wrist, he reached out to wipe the worst of the smudges from her temple.

"Cleaner than my hands," he said. "Don't worry. I've had all my shots."

He felt linked to her, briefly light and sure of himself despite their situation. They were starting to click like a team, a very different team from the one he and Sam had been. He rested his hand on her shoulder.

"You're damned good," he said. "I don't think I've ever told you that."

She smiled.

Ellery started to wonder how much attention he was likely to attract getting into the lodge and up the elevator. His shirt was torn and he wore ground-in dust from collar to sneakers. His jacket was wrapped around his hand to hide the .38 he held in readiness.

Over Channing's shoulder he surveyed the lobby. No sign of anyone who should put them immediately on their guard . . .

He stopped, irritation flaring and waning again, as he realized it probably wasn't her doing. Not any more than Serafin's stowing away. The woman in front of him simply inspired loyalties on a different level than most people did. He'd have to accept it.

"One thing," he said slowly, amusement nudging against the tension inside him. "Could you at least spare me the white rabbits?"

She frowned in puzzlement, then turned to follow his gaze. Ellery heard her teeth grind as she spotted the bent, hook-nosed form of her houseman.

Eighteen

Rundell unfolded his stooped frame from a lobby couch with amazing alacrity. By the time Channing heard the entry door whoosh shut behind her, he was tottering in a beeline toward her, his expression more puckered than usual, a critical glint in his eye. She felt, for some reason that mystified her, like a kid caught skipping school.

"Rundell!" she said in a hiss. "What the hell are you doing here?"

"Finding out what the hell you want with a card shaver, madam." His teeth snapped shut. He scowled. "When has a Stuart ever cheated at cards? When has a Stuart ever needed to mark cards for a trick—"

"I ought to can you!" Channing said, interrupting, almost as annoyed by his misjudgment of her as she was by his appearance here. "I need it to repair a piece of apparatus—and I needed it this morning, dammit!"

From the corner of her eye she could see Wilbur peering out the door to his office. No doubt Rundell had cut quite a figure inquiring for her. Serafin, his expression one of commiseration, scuttled past Wilbur and started toward them.

"Rubbish," said Rundell. His teeth clicked again. At least he had the decency to keep his voice to a whisper, Channing thought. She held out her hand. With a sniff Rundell handed her the small envelope she knew to be the card shaver.

Serafin scooted to a stop behind her elbow.

"I tried to tell him everything was mellow, but he wouldn't leave," the boy said desperately.

He and Rundell glared at each other.

"I'm due a vacation, madam." Rundell's tone was truculent. "It's been eight years since—"

"Yes. Fine. Stay, by all means."

The best way to deal with Rundell had always been to keep him off-balance. Arguing would get her nowhere. Sobered by the knowledge of what she and Ellery were facing, and aware that she was losing time that could be vital, she pressed ahead.

"Check in if you haven't already."

There was always the chance Rundell could prove useful. He kept his head about things. She'd feel more certain of Serafin's safety with him around too. Crooking her arm through Rundell's, she started toward the elevators.

"I want Serafin to stay with you tonight. Don't do anything or go anywhere without clearing it with me. And don't say anything about seeing one of the men who came to the house. It could cost him—or me—our lives. Do you understand?"

"Perfectly, madam." Rundell's hooked nose had raised majestically. He was practically smirking. "Why do you think I showed up here? Only a blithering idiot would believe that crap about a charity gig. I knew you were getting yourself into some sort of mess."

* * *

"I didn't hear a thing," Walker mumbled. "Had those earphones on—is he going to be okay?"

He was holding his head, the plump lines of his face like the underbelly of a thundercloud. Ellery knelt over Max's prostrate form, a cold washcloth pressed to the back of Max's head.

"Yeah, looks like just the same as you got. I don't suppose you found anything in Ballieu's room?"

Walker scowled.

"Not diddly-squat. And no one showed up for a pickup, either."

He sounded defensive.

Ellery nodded. He'd found them both sprawled unconscious. It had taken several minutes to bring Walker around. Now there was a knock at the door. Muttering under his breath, Walker rose to check the peephole and let Channing enter.

"How'd we do?" she asked almost gaily. "I stayed for a drink with somebody after the show. I thought it might look better than coming straight up. My God, you're filthy, Ellery! What did you get into out there?"

Somehow the dishevelment of her hair seemed deliberate, Ellery marveled. She carried her jacket slung casually across her shoulder. Substantial as it had been, the ripped seam wasn't apparent. For half a second Ellery wondered if she'd switched the garment or turned it inside out or actually had some trick for restoring things. Then he recognized it must have something to do with the way she'd folded it, and her inherent showmanship.

"Max and Walker both got beaned on the back of

the head, and things didn't go much better for me." Ellery thought they played well together. He shared a look with her, wondering how much of what he'd found here was true. Beneath the outer brightness of her eyes he could see she was thinking the same.

A groan gurgled out as Max began to come to.

"Take it easy," Ellery said.

Max's eyes fluttered open. He saw Ellery, squinted, then blinked in confusion.

"What—?"

Once again Ellery felt his gaze being drawn to Channing's. Could either of the men in this room be acting?

"Looks like we got ambushed all around," he said. "I was first prize in a shooting gallery out there."

"I told you I should back you up," said Channing. The tone she adopted now was one shade short of cross. "How'd you get out?"

"Some kid who'd been out taking his girl home." Ellery grinned. "Saw one too many movies, I guess. Heard a couple of shots and headed his truck right in to see the action."

Infrared was good enough to pinpoint a vehicle but not to identify it beyond a vague shape. His story should hold.

"A kid in a truck?" sputtered Walker.

Max was pulling himself to a sitting position, a hand to the base of his skull. Channing pointed suddenly to the monitor showing the door to Ballieu's room.

"Look!"

His profile to them, Ballieu was unlocking the

door. He went inside. Max was squinting again. He stared at the screen. His mouth was agape.

"You trying to tell us Ballieu's on to us?" he asked.

No eye contact, Ellery noted. He hated watching men he'd worked with as though they were criminals.

"Looks like it," he said.

"Then why would he come back?"

"Because he's smart, man." Walker sounded irritable. "He can't get the film because it's locked up somewhere with a time bomb. He's waiting us out." Taking a fresh cigar, he stuffed the end into his mouth. "Ballieu figures even if he'd picked one of us off tonight, we'd leave him be until he led us to that film."

"Crazy bastard," Max grunted, staggering to his feet. "Must have nerves of steel." He winced and gave Ellery a glum look. "Now what?"

"I'd say we might as well sleep on it," said Ellery mildly. Too mildly? he wondered. Both men were staring at him. "I'll be in at four to take the graveyard shift."

Channing shrugged as though concluding nothing of consequence was likely to happen and drifted out ahead of him. She deserved double credit, Ellery thought, first for what she'd done tonight and then for not having it recognized.

"We'd better get rid of my car," she said when he'd closed the door and they started down the hall in step together. "If someone gets a good look at the shape it's in, they're likely to call the police."

"I've already put in a call about it," he said.

"While I was waiting for Walker to come around. Somebody will take it away and bring mine in."

His mind was moving in other directions as he spoke. Ballieu must be feeling pressured to have sprung the ambush, and with time slipping by and the knowledge he was being watched, he might strike again.

Ellery slanted a look at the woman beside him, hardening himself with a discipline he knew was necessary. He watched her eyes darken as he spoke.

"Come get the gun."

Nineteen

They moved across the now nearly deserted terraces and down the path to Ellery's bungalow in silence. On a bench a pair of lovers were scanning the stars for the Big Dipper. Cool night air permeated the plants and shadows. The noisy resort had changed personalities, becoming soft and oasislike, and Channing felt the irony of knowing the world she and Ellery moved in was a world apart.

Beside her Ellery moved at an easy, unhurried pace she sensed was deceiving. The wadded jacket was carried too casually in his hand. Despite her own sharpened alertness, she felt almost light. Oddly, the weariness that should be settling in after tonight's wear and tear had evaporated in a strange flow of energy. She stopped as Ellery motioned to her. His eyes analyzed every detail of the bungalow door before he opened it. For a moment she shivered, alone, while he slipped inside.

Then lights came on and he beckoned to her, holding the door. He locked it behind them.

"Receiver for a homing device we've got in Ballieu's car," he said, unlocking and opening an attaché case that sat on a table. "Reception's better out here than it is in the main building, and of course the initial idea was that I'd be out here guarding you."

All those precautions for nothing, Channing thought. She met Ellery's eyes and, by the anger there, knew that as one they were facing an ugly truth.

"Which one is it?" she asked. "Max or Walker?"

He rested his hands on either side of the attaché case, leaning heavily on the table. His face looked tired.

"I don't know. How could either of them knock the other out, drive to those rocks, and be back ahead of us? That had to be Ballieu out there—and he wasn't alone."

"I'd have guessed a small army myself."

He smiled, but only briefly.

"At least two people, judging by the angle of the shots. They had night scopes."

She ran fingers through her tangled hair.

"Oliver?"

"Could be."

The admission stuck in Ellery's throat. Not Oliver. Oliver had given him his first field assignment. Oliver had sprung him from that hospital. Oliver had worried over him at times like a goddamn mother hen.

But when he'd radioed in a little while ago to report the ambush and get the cars straightened out, Oliver hadn't been there. Out picking up sandwiches, someone had said.

He tried to think on the basis of pure reason, untouched by emotion, and was grateful Channing gave him the space, not speaking but waiting. Was there anything else to incriminate Oliver besides his absence at almost the same time Ellery had been dodging gunfire? Any minuscule slip that Ellery should have noted? Any change in behavior?

Looked at that way, the whole operation was a deviation. It had been uncharacteristic of Oliver to bring in someone totally untrained and unknown, as Channing was. It was almost whimsical. Ditto the plan he'd hatched. But then Ballieu was behaving equally out of character if he had a helper, as Ellery believed now more than ever. Maybe breaking a pattern when stakes were high wasn't deviation so much as genius, the sort of thing that made a man on either side excel.

"It could be somebody over Oliver too," said Ellery. "If a person knew who to sell it to, that film would bring enough to tempt anyone."

There was the dilemma. It might be pointless going over Oliver's head, and he was no longer sure he could trust the man himself.

"And everyone who's involved right now knew Yussuf had contacts?" Channing asked slowly.

He nodded.

"Walker's as tense as a tomcat and flaking out to make those phone calls to his daughter—supposedly. Max's digestive upset could have been faked."

Straightening, he went into the bathroom and began to wash grime from his face and hands. Channing followed to stand in the doorway.

"Max and Walker don't know the whole story, but if it's Oliver or someone else up the line, then Ballieu knows exactly what you're planning," he said.

"Then I'll do something else."

Ellery was fighting a battle inside himself. Let her, or try to get her out of it? He'd thought his mind was made up when he'd asked her to help. Seeing her standing there with her growing determination made him waver.

"What's the alternative?" she asked vigorously. "Give up the film? You don't know who you can trust, and you can't outmaneuver Ballieu all by yourself! That's why I'm here now, isn't it?"

He brushed past her, avoiding her eyes. He could feel his throat contracting. They were just individuals. What they could accomplish was more important than either of them. And she understood that.

Out of habit he emptied his pockets, tossing down his wallet and rubbing his thumb across the old gold watch before he set it almost reverently on the nightstand. There might be a better way now than letting Channing do her sleight of hand, but the only chance to avoid it depended on uncovering the mole in their midst. Either that or they'd have to locate—and get to—the film.

He opened the drawer and reached under a Gideon Bible.

"Know how to load this?" he asked, handing her the small .38 and a box of ammunition.

She nodded wordlessly. He knew she recognized the danger now.

"A friend in La Paz insisted on teaching me once."

"Smart man."

For most of his adult years and beyond, he'd never let himself need anyone, because as a kid he'd never *had* anyone. Now his longing to reach for her was a growing ache. The way she answered his sharpness with teasing. Her laughter. The way she looked directly at him and didn't turn away.

He gathered her to him and found her mouth. He could feel the self-control that had seemed such an integral part of her shattering with his. He wound his hand through the spicy tangles of her hair and knew this—this moment—was one of the reasons, maybe even the prime reason, he'd never wanted to be involved with her.

His kiss was harder than any Channing had ever experienced. Nothing like Tony. Never had she thrown caution to the wind so defiantly. Her abandonment of all composure frightened her. Yet with Ellery, as they gripped and held each other, she knew a total freedom, the certainty of the universe, and her direction in it that had eluded her too long.

Her fingers, pressed tightly against his back, touched the thin leather strap of his holster. In her other hand, turned carefully away, she could feel the menacing heaviness of the gun she held. Reminders that this might never happen again.

She closed out everything but the present moment. This was what it meant being an adult, she thought, knowing how things changed and valuing their brief glimmer. It was Ellery who disengaged himself, still holding her tightly. His eyes fought to hide his vulnerability. He was as shaken by the collapse of discipline between them as she was herself.

"I was right not to want you working on this," he said slowly. "But for all the wrong reasons." His fingers traced the side of her face. "Come on. I'll walk you back."

She could tell by the tautness of his body that he

wanted to make love to her. She leaned back in his arms.

"Do you work at insulting me, Ellery, or does it come naturally?" The teasing caught in her throat.

He shook his head, and she read in the gesture and the hard set of his face a self-denial.

"Chances are at least one of us won't come out of this. Let's not make it worse."

She remembered the pain of losing Tony. Except she knew now that having nothing to lose was more painful still.

"Nothing's guaranteed. I learned that a long time ago. But it's not a reason to stop living. It's why every minute counts!"

For a moment she thought she'd won. His fingers dug into her. He kissed her again. When he released her, she saw in the tightness at the edge of his eyes the discipline it cost him and matched it with her own. No words were needed between them.

They couldn't allow themselves this luxury. It would make them both too vulnerable. Responsibility came ahead of personal desires. She'd known it but had yielded for a moment. Now her eyes tried to telegraph that she had herself under control. She didn't want to make things harder. She drew a breath.

"Well. Do I go keep an eye on Max and Walker, or what?"

Her voice had an artificial sound. Ellery still hadn't let go of her arms. He seemed to be rallying too.

"I don't suppose you've ever been invited to go

over computer forms in a man's hotel room," he said.

"You'd be surprised what I've been asked to do."

He grinned.

"I'll bet I would. Just remind me never to let you drive a car of mine."

"I thought you came from money, Ellery. Changed cars as often as flower arrangements."

"Past tense. Maybe I'll tell you about it sometime."

"I saw a picture of your brother in the paper. He looks like a jerk."

"He is a jerk."

For a moment Channing wondered if she'd been wrong about that flash of urgency she'd felt between them earlier. Still, something had changed, and these words that were inconsequential on the surface were a part of it.

Ellery stepped away to open a drawer.

"There's some data to comb through that might put us ahead of Ballieu and whoever he's working with," he said, removing a stack of fan-folded printouts. "Not exactly authorized, but I brought a computer and used it to get information on all the real estate that was rented or sold around here in the last three months. If we could find a place that might have a safe, or a name we recognized, we might be on to something. It'd go faster with two people."

His eyebrows raised.

Equals. A new stage. Channing pulled a chair toward the bed, kicked her shoes off, and sat down, propping her feet up.

"I've always been a sucker for glamour."

He tossed her the top half of the printout and pulled a chair up facing hers. Settling into it, he tipped back on the rear legs.

"Yeah, well. When the glamour starts to overwhelm you, I'll order coffee."

On the nightstand, the slender hands of Ellery's old gold pocket watch showed that it was after one A.M. Whatever success or failure they were destined for was going to have to come today.

At three A.M. Henri Ballieu rose to wash his face and slake a raging thirst. Sleep was eluding him. The scent of success, the moment when the task entrusted to him would be completed, was too clear in his nostrils for his nerves to unwind. And the pain inside him was rising, traveling a new, hot arc from the spot in his belly to his head. He stood and let himself experience it fully, its depth, its frequency. To become familiar with an enemy was to insure victory.

In darkness he removed the gun hidden under his mattress, reduced it into assorted parts, and reassembled it, satisfied with its perfect cleanness. If a man couldn't work in the dark in Ballieu's occupation, he would not last long. Ballieu often rose by night, especially in new surroundings, and sat until his eyes could pick out minute details and his ears identify the slightest sounds.

His nimble fingers fitted a silencer onto the tip of the gun, then removed it, testing, checking. There was no such thing as too much caution. He might well need to use the weapon several times by the time it turned dark again and the hired helicopter picked him up with the film in his pocket.

The American agent, Ellery, was very good. He had gone belly-down in the ambush as well as Ballieu could have himself.

What had gone wrong? Who had helped the American? It angered Ballieu that he had no answers. He had been promised that all the other Americans would be occupied. He was starting to lose confidence in the seller. But these were challenges, and Ballieu liked a challenge.

He felt suddenly hungry. The dinner he had eaten had come up hours ago out there in the rocks. Bad meat. He ought to complain.

Now his tongue craved eggs on a bed of asparagus with a rich sauce over it. Some freshly squeezed juice. Thoughts of food and other physical comforts had begun to possess him of late. He was starting to be tempted by mortal things. Why? What was making him greedy? There would be time enough to eat or stare at a painting or feel the sun on his back next week . . . next year . . .

Ballieu felt a frantic, repetitive scratching at the edge of his brain that had nothing to do with the pain in his belly, nothing to do with the job ahead of him. The fire inside him traveled its circuit again, and he touched fingers to the cold sweat standing out on his upper lip.

He could take something for the pain—he had a packet of potent tablets in his shaving kit. But they would dull his senses. He had to remain alert. He had to keep a close watch on the female sent to help him. She pretended meekness now, but he didn't trust her.

Pressing a hand to his side, Ballieu picked up the telephone and ordered food. He felt a passing sympathy for Khadija. So young and intense. He remembered being like that, though he had disciplined himself where she did not. He remembered, too, the burden he'd borne as a child for being a bastard. It engendered a brief guilt in his mind. But then perhaps the situation was easier for a girl.

He thought of his pampered cousin, Muhammed. What would have become of him by now?

He thought about knowing a woman.

He wondered why the past kept suddenly coming back to him.

Ballieu rose, cursing the thoughts that distracted him. He stretched and squatted to loosen the spreading tenderness along his side. Years from now, students of revolution would study how Henri Ballieu had slipped through Americans' fingers in their own territory. He had proved himself at sixteen. Now, when some thought him too old, when his own body sought to betray him, he was going to prove himself all over again.

Coolly Ballieu thought through, once more, every move remaining for getting the film. Today.

Bill Ellery stood, as the minutes of early morning ticked by, and looked at the woman asleep in his chair. He'd never wanted to make love to a woman so badly in his life. He wanted to hold her, to explore her with no barriers between them. The mysteries she performed onstage were nothing compared to the mystery of the woman herself.

He thought of waking her, then knew it would only make it harder to leave. It had been hard enough saying no to her last night, worse still saying no to himself. For he'd known if he held her, if he had her even for an hour, it would make up for all the things he'd missed in his life.

She was warm. Unpredictable. A thousand things he didn't understand. He brushed the hair back from the scratch on her temple, let his fingers linger, and debated moving her onto the bed.

If he left her where she was, she'd have one hell of a crick in her neck when she woke up. If he lifted her, he might wake her. She'd worked like a trooper, cool and rational when he'd valued that most. They'd narrowed his list down to a few leads he could follow up. He hadn't even realized she'd fallen asleep till he'd asked a question and she hadn't answered. Now he was due at the listening post, and she deserved some decent rest.

He stooped and lifted her and found her lighter than he'd expected. It must be the loose clothes she favored. Or the fact that she didn't make a point of being delicate, so the slightness, the slenderness, of her form escaped notice. She moved with such competence and had so much pepper about her, the fact that she was a desirable woman was easy to overlook sometimes. She probably planned it that way. He grinned.

She stirred in his arms but didn't awaken. Ellery thought how he'd like to take care of her precisely because she didn't seem to need it; how loving her would be an act between equals.

He thought how he'd like to see this day over, even with Ballieu escaping. His mouth pulled down at the traitorous thought. He'd keep reminding himself of Sam's death—even though Sammy, of all people, would have understood this opposite tug he was feeling.

It was light outside.

Channing should be as safe in this room as she'd be anywhere else here, especially with him out and visible. Just to be certain, he loaded her .38 and put it behind a rumpled-up fold of the bedspread. It was where she would see it immediately. And it pointed toward the door.

Twenty

Channing had floated up several layers, away from the deepest part of sleep. Her brain, still in a lazy state, nonetheless recorded sounds nearby. Her door was being opened carefully, almost stealthily. She came alert, remembering where she was, remembering danger. Her opening eyes saw the gun. She reached for it.

"Channing?"

It was Serafin. Whispering.

"Brought you some coffee."

Still prone, she felt relief dampen her skin and eased her finger away to safety. She buried the gun in a fold of bedspread, out of Serafin's sight.

Nice work, Ellery, she thought wryly. *Except you gave me credit for better reflexes than I have.*

Groggily she sat up, not much worried by the thought of what might have happened if her reflexes had been better. Nothing would have happened. She couldn't use a gun unless she knew herself to be in mortal danger. It was a fact she simply knew about herself.

"It's after eight," she said in disbelief. "How'd you know where to find me? How'd you get in?"

Serafin looked pleased with himself as he moved toward the bed with a tray held before him.

"Just told the desk I needed the key for this bungalow. The day clerk's not as swift as the night clerk. Didn't even look suspicious. I'll have to mention it to Wilbur. Sloppy security."

"I see you're really soaking up the hotel management," she said, taking the tray with an enthusiasm she didn't try to contain. She lifted a lid, and the robust fragrance of coffee began to revive her. She sighed.

Serafin was eyeing her clothes.

"You and Ellery worked all night, huh? Too bad." He sounded disappointed.

Channing gave him a narrow look over her coffee cup. He perched on the foot of the bed and reached for the second pot of coffee. She smacked his hand.

"Aw, Channing, don't give me that line about coffee stunting my growth. Don't you know nothing about Third World countries?"

"Anything. And yes, I'm aware you probably had it in your baby bottle because it was cheaper than milk. But you don't need it at your age. And I do."

He shrugged and let the subject drop, which reassured Channing that he must have had breakfast already. Most likely more than once, in view of the hour.

"So who's winning?" he asked, flopping back easily. "Us or the bad guys?"

It disturbed her a little, the way he zeroed in more than he should on what was happening. He veered back and forth between precocious and typical twelve-year-old. She decided not to discard the reply that sprang to her lips.

"I think it's what's commonly known as a Mexican

standoff," she said, and hid behind her coffee cup before her mouth twitched.

Serafin looked at her with disdain.

"You're not gonna bug me with that. I'm as Yankee as they come now. Legal and everything."

"Where's Rundell?"

"Sunning himself. Boy, his toes are as crooked as that beak of his. He thinks you shacked up with Ellery. Hasn't even called your room yet. He's being discreet. Hey—where are you going?"

He jackknifed up as she slid off the bed, stepped into her shoes, and stuffed her gun and extra ammunition into a dry-cleaning bag. Channing picked up the second pot of coffee and the key to her own room.

"Up to shower and change. Then riding."

"Riding—you mean horses?"

All evidence of Ellery's computer and the printouts they'd pored over last night had vanished, but she had several nearby locations fixed in her mind.

"That's right."

"Can I come?" asked Serafin, trotting at her heels. Any thoughts of danger had vanished for him now, lost in the prospect of a good time.

Channing considered. It might be a good idea. It would look more innocent than her going out alone. If she found anyplace that looked promising, she could send him on back.

"Yes," she said, "but first find Rundell. Tell him if he sees Ellery to pass the word we'll be out to the north of here. And have Rundell rustle me up a camera and a telephoto lens."

She started to heft the small coffeepot she'd set

down momentarily, but it crashed to the floor as her right hand convulsed with a cramp.

"What's wrong?" Serafin's eyes were wide as he followed it.

"Nothing." She ground the word out. "Just clumsy."

Her tendons had jerked a second, a third, half a dozen times. She was suddenly clammy. Nothing had ever afflicted her hands before. Had her practice been too intense? Was something wrong? Could it happen again?

"Do the bit with Rundell. Then bring me some more coffee, will you? And toast and an egg."

The calm of her voice swirled in her ears.

As she turned away from Serafin she opened and closed her hand. It caused a small ache.

It would pass. It had to pass, she told herself. Too much depended on her. She had to help Ellery. She had to perform the job she'd been sent to perform. She had to prove to herself that she was a Stuart.

The foothills around the resort were bleak and dry, hardly scenic by the stretch of anyone's imagination. Half an hour's ride north of the resort, just across a dusty asphalt road, the terrain grew rough. Harder to reach than some of the pieces of property on Ellery's list that were on the highway to the nearest town, and yet more isolated. Channing couldn't think why anyone would erect a building in such a locale unless they had terminal asthma or were running drugs. Yet according to Ellery's information there must be a few plots of real estate hidden away back here. Vacation homes. Year-round homes, maybe, for those after lower taxes than they'd pay in a city.

She reined in her horse. Her right hand rested loosely on her thigh, and it felt almost normal. Almost. Not completely. The camera, with its long, heavy lens, was leaving a sweaty streak under the band that held it. They'd been out for over an hour. Serafin squinted at her, his nose wrinkling.

"Come on, Channing. What're we hunting?"

Deliberately—and out of wariness—she'd been keeping all her senses tuned to the surroundings, leaving little room for thoughts about the object of her search. Now she sighted through the camera again, as she'd done periodically.

"I thought you read minds," she said.

He cocked his head.

"You're doing something to make it hard."

She still didn't answer. Was that a deliberate line she saw winding in the distance?

Letting the camera down, she nudged her mount.

"Let's ride up that way."

They climbed higher, Serafin's horse resisting the effort at times. He wasn't an expert rider. Channing started to wonder if she'd been grasping at straws coming out here. Then the horses wheezed up a dusty ridge, and ahead of them lay a rough private drive. It twisted still higher. Whatever might wait at the top was screened from the probing of Channing's camera by the landscape itself, a hodgepodge of boulders and steep angles. Hiding frustration, she assessed the drive again. It gave an obvious vantage point to anyone at the top. She was turning her horse when a metal plate fixed in one of the near boulders caught her eye.

"Desert View Clinic," read Serafin as they rode closer.

A scrubby little bush had taken root in a crack in the rock and was starting to obscure the sign. The Desert View Clinic didn't look open for business.

Channing felt her pulse quickening. This was the break they needed, maybe. The kind of place that might have had a vault once, for patients' valuables or medicine.

"Let's get back," she said.

Avoiding the drive, she led the way back down toward an outcrop of rock. She was planning. Tell Ellery what she'd found. This was one of the places on his list, and it certainly looked promising. If nothing else turned up—

She rounded the outcrop and jerked on her reins so sharply that the horse beneath her reared. She was face-to-face with Henri Ballieu. He, too, was on horseback, and he had a gun with a silencer leveled at her. At *us,* she amended sickly, hearing Serafin's gasp at her flank.

"Looking for something?" Ballieu's voice held a deceptive pleasantness.

In a split second Channing decided, almost intuitively, how she had to play this.

"I'm looking for you, Ballieu," she said as smoothly as he had. "Was your meeting last night successful?" She gave a velvety smile as the pupils of his eyes widened almost indiscernibly. Knowing how to read an audience, how to judge a reaction, was paying off. "I put something in your watch," she said. "I thought I should . . . know you better. Haven't you discovered it?"

It was, she theorized, the last thing in the world he'd expect her to say. But maybe what someone who aspired to take over a business like Yussuf's would really do. By volunteering exactly what he'd meant to confront her with, she'd made him uncertain. She let her eyes flick suggestively to the surrounding rocks.

"Put the gun away, Ballieu. Do you think we'd come here alone? Yussuf's people—*my* people—have been watching this place since before you arrived."

He looked cunning now, and it made her own confidence waver.

"And the one you left up there who's dead?"

Damn. This could be a test. Or had he been up there . . . killed whoever was guarding the place? But he couldn't have gotten the film or he wouldn't still be here wasting time with her.

She shrugged.

"We're testing each other, Ballieu. We both know it."

All the time she could hardly swallow, trying not to watch his gun, trying not to think of Serafin in the middle of this.

Ballieu switched his horse around. Coming nearer. Half circling her. The gun didn't waver.

"You're bluffing," he said. "You don't know where the film is and you're hunting it."

Wrong, she thought. *You're confirming what I need to know.*

Calmly, pretending indifference to him with every ounce of acting skill she'd ever acquired, Channing reached up and removed the camera from around her neck. She shook her hair back.

"If you knew as much about me as I know about you, you'd know I'm a geologist. I'm fascinated by rock formations." She gave a provocative smile. "Good cover for the kind of work I did for Yussuf, don't you think?"

Steeling herself, she turned to Serafin and handed him the camera.

"Take this back for me. I have business to talk over."

Serafin's dark eyes met hers and received the message to do more than just take it back. He'd take it straight to Ellery and tell him what had happened. She felt sure of it. She hit his horse on the rump.

Ballieu veered, on the verge of stopping the boy, but she spoke again.

"There are federal agents watching you, Ballieu. Do we cooperate?"

Once more she'd startled him, made another crack in his distrust of her if she was lucky. His gun dipped slightly.

"How do you know who's watching me?"

His eyes were narrow. Accusing. Yet wavering in their certainty. Channing looked at him with what she hoped was guile.

"I have my ways."

She could feel the two of them in double checkmate, will against will, wit against wit, her personality locked with his. A gleam she couldn't identify touched his eyes. He studied her and slid his tongue across his lower lip.

"Yussuf's people aren't happy about your killing him," she continued. "But they'll do whatever I tell them. If I walk out with you when you get the film, they'll accept our truce. If not . . . Can you see behind all these rocks?"

He chuckled suddenly, a chilling sound. He brought his horse closer to hers. His gun was lowered.

"And if I agree to a truce, what more?" His hand ran up the side of her throat. "There'll be more than business, perhaps? You entice me." His fingers turned over to stroke the faint line of her windpipe.

Channing felt her flesh crawl. Sensuality and the threat of death mingled in his touch.

"We'll see," she said, struggling to maintain her poise.

He moved back. He slid the gun into a pocket, unwrapped a red-and-white candy, and dropped the cellophane on the ground. An expression like amusement curled his mouth.

"Be at the small pool at midnight," he said. "We'll go from there."

As she started to leave, the small of her back still prickling, he caught her reins.

"If anything goes wrong—if you've lied to me—you won't walk out, either."

Hate, like the dark sides of a box, closed around her. She couldn't touch him. She couldn't betray the contempt she felt. Yet she wouldn't bow beneath the fear he generated, either.

"I hope you're better dressed at midnight," she said. "That flower you're wearing's too gaudy."

The outrush of his breath was audible as he looked down to see the orange paper flower projecting from his shirt pocket. He realized she'd placed it there, and he hurled it angrily to the ground.

It had been an act of defiance causing it to appear there, an act she realized she should have resisted yet didn't regret. Channing spun, setting her course toward the resort, deliberately not looking over her shoulder.

Twenty-one

"See Ballieu out there?" Walker, none too firm in his saddle, galloped up as Channing reached the stable area. "He gave me the slip."

From half a dozen lengths behind them, Ellery saw Channing slide to the ground and nod in answer. She paid no attention as Walker took off in pursuit. As though attempting to steady herself, she bowed her forehead against the side of the horse she'd ridden.

Tension easing, Ellery swung his own horse close. Her face was pale, but she looked unharmed. Her eyes sprang open.

"I know where the film is," she said, breathing hard.

"Old mental hospital on long-term lease to some movie company?" He spoke quickly, keeping part of his attention on Walker's retreating figure while his horse danced impatiently. "Serafin told me. Said you'd run into Ballieu and he'd pulled a gun—"

"It's okay. He's taking me up there at midnight—"

"He could be lying. I'm going to keep my eye on Walker. Back me up."

He gave his horse its head and lunged ahead. They had lost several seconds in conversation. Now, as he reached the outer gate of the stable area, he saw Walker already circling back. Another dot farther out was heading in as well. Wheeling, Ellery trotted back and dismounted, watching Channing, just up in her saddle again, do likewise.

"We look like the goddamn cavalry," he said in disgust.

"Real subtle, huh?"

"Yeah."

Her mouth had twisted sidewise, reflecting an irony similar to his own. The shared recognition of absurdity made him feel better, even knowing their backs were against the wall. Smacking the horses on their rumps, he sent them toward the stable.

"I thought maybe Walker was our man, and the meeting going down now. But they're both coming in," he said.

"So it's not Walker?"

Ellery squinted, wishing he could see the answer.

"Who knows? Maybe we were just too close behind." He brought his gaze back from the horizon. "I'd dug up some facts of my own before Serafin found me. It was under a phony name, of course, but Yussuf subleased that old clinic about a week ago. The check number traced back to an account he kept."

She was quiet. He knew it still hurt her, facing the fact that a man she'd valued as friend had been what Yussuf was.

"You'd never make it up there in daylight, Ellery," she said with a waver in the steadiness of her voice. "The place has an open view of everything moving below. And guards. I think Ballieu killed one."

He nodded, lost in thought.

"We'll gamble on your meeting at midnight then, unless there's movement beforehand."

They started back toward the grounds of the lodge. Ellery looked at her, eyes traveling the length of her body.

"You have strings and things under the costume you wear for your act?"

Her eyes took on a teasing look. She grinned without answering.

"Dammit, Channing! I want to know if I can get a wire on you."

Annoyed by her lack of seriousness, he caught her by the wrist and felt her recoil.

"What's wrong?" he asked immediately, releasing her.

Her mouth opened, set for denial.

"Probably an inflamed tendon," said a voice behind them. "Doesn't have any better sense than her father did when he found a new pair of handcuffs."

They turned as one.

Channing's houseman was padding toward them, his body set at an angle. It was as white as grits, with lumps where his knees should be and chartreuse swim trunks flapping above them like curtains. His misshaped nose was in the air. Serafin was beside him.

"All this practicing 'round the clock all of a sudden," he lectured, a narrowed eye on his employer. "Using muscles you'd let get flabby. You're out of shape, you know, madam, and you're not a girl anymore. Let me see." He poked the exact spot to make her gasp. "Rest and aspirin. I'm going to tape it to keep you from using it."

Ellery entertained a fleeting thought that the household help where he'd grown up, afraid of overstepping bounds and being dismissed, wouldn't even have ventured advice on what to wear outside on a rainy day.

"Beat it, Rundell," said Channing between her teeth. "It's nothing. I bumped it on something."

"Rubbish. The boy already told me you dropped your coffeepot this morning."

The old bird had a lot of steel inside him, Ellery decided. And Ellery shared his hunch that Channing wasn't telling the truth about her condition. They were breaking the rules enough as it was, and her flawless performance was vital. He looked at the houseman.

"You know what you're talking about?"

The old man drew himself almost erect.

"I was The Great Sebastian's assistant for fifteen years."

Ellery gave a nod.

"She'll wait for you in the lobby."

He whisked Channing aside before she could protest, and before Rundell could unhinge his mouth to speak again.

"I'm trusting your judgment," he said, his voice lowered. "If a point comes when you think you can't do the job, speak up for chrissake. Otherwise it's the two of us against Ballieu and whoever. For practical purposes we have to consider Max, Walker, and Oliver—all three—the enemy."

"That spreads us thin."

A family with three children came bustling toward them, heading for the stable and chattering happily about the ride they'd have. Ellery didn't answer.

"I'm still convinced Ballieu's got a helper too," he said when the family had passed. He wished he could forget that Ballieu had been known to snatch people around him for cover.

"So our agenda for today is?"

"Try to spot the mole. Try to spot the helper. Failing that, let's play it as planned and hope we move fast."

He glanced at her as they walked beneath the thin shadow cast by a palm tree. To the right there were shouts from a doubles game on one of the tennis courts.

"I'm not taking chances with you, Channing. That's why I want you wired. I'm going to be within fifty yards of you all the time, if possible. The minute you see anyone familiar, you go to ground and I'll move in."

"Along with whoever's on our side, once they see the lay of the land?"

"Let's hope so. If you were really playing the game you want Ballieu to think you are, you wouldn't tell any of the rest of us about the meeting you've set with him. So I'll wait till the last minute to call the others in.

"The main thing is, forget the film switch. Save your hide. We'll have our traitor."

"And Ballieu."

"Right."

"And if I *don't* see anyone I thought was on our side, then I play it through?"

"Yeah. I guess. Just be prepared to duck for cover. And, Channing—don't hesitate to use the artillery."

They had come to a crossroad where one branch of the sidewalk led toward the noise and activity of the main pool area, another branch to the lodge itself. He halted. A crossroad. For one split second he considered how simple it would be for the two of them to walk out, get into a car, and drive away—or walk into Oliver's post and announce they had a traitor somewhere and even get a pat on the back.

It stunned him that he'd let his thoughts take such a turn. He touched the shoulder of the woman beside him. There were things he wanted to say, but he merely let his fingers press gently.

"Come in after your first show and I'll put the wire on you," he said. "Until then, keep an eye on whoever's in the listening post."

"And you'll be . . . ?"

"Keeping tabs on Ballieu—and trying to smoke out whoever's with him."

They separated. He glanced back once and saw her testing her hand.

The plastic explosive fit nicely inside one corner of a three-foot-high brick planter. It divided the swimming pool area from a group of tables and was in the middle of things.

How fitting to send a bunch of American pigs to their deaths while they were eating, Khadija thought. She leaned against the planter, the large shoulder bag beside her camouflaging skillful movements of her fingers as she twisted the bomb's detonator into place. She smiled at two fat women who came by, smiled a second time for a waiter who was grinning at her like an idiot as he passed with his tray. Perhaps they would be among the recipients of the gift she was leaving.

It was hard to judge how long it would take the sheath around the detonator to wear through. It ran between two bricks that were loosened. Each shifting of the bricks would wear at its shell.

Khadija had noticed people were always perching on the edge of the planter. Girls who were flirting with men. Men who were watching for girls. Children. Even as she turned to leave, a group of shrieking boys ran up and jumped on the wall.

This evening, maybe?

Tomorrow?

The brick wasn't loose enough to fall, only to shift itself slightly, its rough bits of dry mortar scraping.

Khadija walked toward the pool to find a chair and sun herself. She would accomplish something against the enemies of her people even if Ballieu didn't.

The leggy blonde whose room Ballieu had visited the day before yesterday was deep in conversation with another man when Ellery spotted her. He waited impatiently. In the next eleven hours Ballieu was bound to move. The knowledge slapped at his chest like a cold, flat meat cleaver that could turn on edge and lay him open at any minute. He had to narrow the odds he and Channing faced. As soon as the other man departed, he moved in.

Though he wore a shirt to hide his bandage, he had changed into swim trunks to blend into the pool scene. He carried a bottle of tanning lotion in his hand.

"The small of your back's red," he announced, dropping into a vacant chair beside the blonde's. She was belly-down, reading a magazine. He displayed his bottle of lotion as she turned her head. "Allow me?"

The blonde gave him a curious once-over.

"Sure. Why not?"

Nice to know all those hours he'd been stuck at the Country Club pool as a kid hadn't been for nothing, Ellery thought. He'd had plenty of chance to observe big brother Reid in action. Reid had been as quick with the lotion then as he was with the oil for constituents now.

The blonde's eyes were alert but didn't seem hostile. Her muscles felt long and relaxed as he smoothed the white cream over her. Her back arched into his hand a little.

"I've seen you around," she said. "You here alone?"

"Yeah."

She had very long fingernails, carefully polished. One of them flipped a page in her magazine. When she felt his hand leave her back, she rolled over and gave him a cynical smile.

"The bartender send you?"

It dawned on Ellery what the lady was. Max had mentioned a call girl, but he'd forgotten it. That, coupled with her response right now, pretty much eliminated her as Ballieu's assistant.

"Afraid not. Do I need a recommendation?" he asked easily.

"Not necessarily."

Her smile widened, showing the tips of her teeth. Ellery said maybe later. Another of Ballieu's conquests, the one with breast-length black hair, was at the far end of the pool.

The lounges near hers were all occupied. Ellery killed twenty minutes. The cleaver at his chest kept pressing harder. Finally, fearing the girl would leave, and seeing she was in the correct facedown position, he decided to move, anyway.

Setting course for a postcard stand, he turned off to walk between chairs. As he passed hers, her head raised. She'd been fully alert, not sunning at all. He stopped and looked back.

"Excuse me," he said. "Did you know your back's getting red? Allow me." He extended the tanning lotion.

Her dark eyes had a scorching quality. Maybe she was just reacting to the obvious come-on. He wouldn't blame her. He'd always thought the girls who responded to Reid's line must be morons.

"I never burn. I love the sun," the girl in front of him said. She looked lean and supple.

Her English was very good. Almost no accent. And the fact that she had one didn't prove anything.

"You sure?" pressed Ellery. "It'd be a shame to see such a lovely back sunburned."

If she was connected with Ballieu, she should have sense enough to play along in hopes of throwing him off-guard. His eyes watched hers. They told him nothing.

"If you insist," she said with boredom. She lay back down.

Ellery stepped closer and squirted a line of lotion into his hand. He smoothed it along her spine. Her muscles were tensed for action and as hard as ropes. There was always a chance they were well developed because she was some sort of dancer or acrobat. But Ellery doubted it.

"I read somewhere that brunettes are more susceptible to sunburn than other women," he said. "Do you think that's true?"

Old Reid's best poolside routine. Used on a terrorist.

Because Ellery was sure now that was what she was. He wouldn't need to interview any more of Ballieu's female companions. He'd had a chance to look at this one's hands.

The nails were stylishly manicured. Her skin was soft with lotion, and a crash course of attention. Beneath the surface smoothness, though, on her palms and fingers, he could see calluses. She hadn't gotten them from ironing or doing charcoal sketches, either. They were in the exact location, the exact spots where they'd develop from rigorous training with an assault rifle.

Twenty-two

The child ran into him, her flying arms tangled around his leg.

"Oops. Careful, little one," Ballieu laughed, resting a hand on her head. It was damp, the curls still soft with a baby's silkiness. He liked the feel.

The little girl looked up at him with great dark eyes. She came just above his knee.

"I'm going to see my grandpa next week," she piped, tugging at the top strip of her two-piece bathing suit. "He lives in Rome."

Ballieu smiled. She was an engaging little girl, the sort who would be a delight to hold on your knee and entertain with stories. He hoped she wouldn't be blown up by one of the bombs Khadija's group planned to install in international airports using their forged passports—but children had to die like everyone else.

"I'll bet your grandpa takes you to the park, eh? And buys you candies?" Reaching into his pocket, Ballieu handed her a peppermint. "Have this one today."

He watched her take off running again, then turned his attention back to the occupants of the pool and terrace. He was hunting for Mildred Farrow.

Eight hours remained until he began to move. He

wanted to make sure everything was ready. He found the woman he was looking for, plump and pampered, in one of the lodge boutiques. She was chatting vacantly with a salesclerk and fingering a long dress that was all tiers of white muslin trimmed in lace. With motionless eyes Ballieu watched her next try on a thin neck chain holding a nugget of gold. He studied her throat. Strangling her would mean fingers sinking, almost drowning, in perfumed flesh. A blow from the edge of the hand would dispatch her more tidily.

He moved forward. She pivoted on tiny, white-heeled sandals, flushing with delight as she caught sight of him.

"Oh, Harry! The flowers were lovely. You shouldn't have."

"But we won our bridge game yesterday," he said with the hint of a bow. "We deserved to celebrate."

He had ordered an arrangement sent up from the lobby florist. It had paved his way very well. Mildred Farrow, looking both flustered and pleased, unclasped the chain from around her neck.

"I was just being tempted by this. What do you think?"

"It becomes you," said Ballieu.

It was all the urging she needed. He waited while she paid.

"I've had an idea," he said as they strolled into the hall together. "Let's have dinner tonight. In my room. It would be so nice to get away from all these people for a while, don't you think? And their service is very good."

"Well, I—I don't know—"

He hadn't expected her to hesitate. He managed a smile.

"What kind of dinner would you prefer? French? We could still be downstairs in time for the dancing."

There. He had given her opportunity to believe the invitation was wicked or innocent, whichever she preferred. Or to pretend it was one while she hoped it would be the other.

"It *would* be nice to have a meal that was a little quieter," she said.

Ballieu had taken her hand very lightly. She didn't object. Now, very circumspectly, he gave her open palm the lightest brush with his lips.

"This is Oliver Lemming. I'm having my outfit transmit a photograph to you people. We need to know if the lady in it matches anyone in your files—in the next couple hours if you can swing it. We're in a tight spot."

Ellery kept his eyes closed as he spoke into the telephone. Like a damned kid, he thought. As though, if he kept them shut tightly enough, this wouldn't be happening.

The magnitude of his actions was so great, it was starting to lose all reality. Five minutes ago he'd been on a line to State, pretending to be Oliver. Now, forearm thrown against the wall, head bent, he was doing the act all over again. With Interpol, for chrissake!

There was more than giving a name, and he'd known what to say—known Oliver's identification. On the other end of the line he heard affirmation.

"If you find anything, I want you to contact Bill Ellery at the Palacio Sol resort." He gave the number. Where the side of his hand pressed into the wall, he could feel the rough, scratchy texture of wallpaper.

If he was wrong about what was pushing him to this impersonation, he'd lose his job. If he was right, he still might lose it. He was violating the chain of command. He was lying—claiming access to authority he didn't have. It was the only hope he saw for an edge in the situation he and Channing were facing. It was the only way he saw to circumvent and nail a possible traitor.

The worst that could happen was that he'd be out of a job, he thought grimly. He wouldn't let the possibility shove to the front of his mind where it wanted to be. He wouldn't let himself think about what he'd do with the rest of his life if he got tossed out by State. As he shoved away from the wall he also shoved away old doubts from the past.

The phone began to ring before he'd gone three steps. He snatched it up.

"You been on the phone?" asked Oliver, an edge on his voice.

Ellery braced. Oliver was on to him. Maybe Interpol had checked.

"Yeah, to room service," he shot back. He'd make Oliver confront him with it. If Oliver blew up, maybe there'd be something in it to dispel his doubts.

"Anything happening?" asked the man who had hired and trained him.

Ellery felt his nerve endings straining and

stretching, trying to catch any signal that he should trust Oliver or not trust Oliver. He wondered, briefly and heavily, if each of them was screening the other's voice for a clue or a tip-off.

"Nothing happening and no contact," Ellery lied.

"Channing!"

Max waved with a wry, self-mocking hopefulness as he came toward her. He'd realized she didn't like him.

"It's okay," he said, lowering his voice as they met along one side of the vast pool and patio area. "Our man's in his room, and Walker will beep me if he moves." He touched his pocket. "I was going to have a limeade for the old digestion. Want to join me? Looks like we're in the homestretch."

They were standing in front of a long, brick planter. Channing debated. If Max was in league with Ballieu, should she start to play coy, underscore the impression she really had worked for Yussuf, in case he was analyzing? She wasn't quite sure. It was late afternoon. Her hair, piled under a sun hat, felt hot and heavy. She could feel small rivulets of perspiration at her temples.

"Thanks, anyway, but I've got to shower and set up for tonight," she said.

It was too risky trying to second- and third-guess people. She'd better act as she'd always acted with him.

Max hoisted himself up onto the planter. It gave a wonderful view of the pool.

"I don't like the feel of this setup. It's too quiet."

He lifted his face to the sun and pushed at his collar.

His words sounded heavy—as Ellery's had at times. There was a weariness about his movements. It kept Channing from walking on as she might have. Max was easier to take without his ego in full flower.

"I don't see Ellery," he said.

"Neither do I. I guess he's decided I'm a big enough girl to be on my own."

Max gave a single sound of tense amusement. Channing took a step backward, leaning against the planter. She knew Ellery was keeping an eye on her from somewhere—would be till she went inside. One of her fingers traced the bricks behind her. A line of mortar was cracked.

"Things have got to break tonight," Max said, still keeping his voice down. "My guess is they're going to break like hell. Goddamn, but I hate waiting! What's wrong with your hand?"

"Just a little stiffness. The tape's a precaution—to make sure it's in shape for the show." She lifted her arm in a half arc.

The air between them fell silent, an empty gully around which shouts and laughter from the pool washed.

"Channing . . ."

Max sounded strangely hesitant, a quality she hadn't realized he possessed. His eyes, as she looked up, were exposed, stripped of their lazy charm and superficiality. He glanced quickly away. For the first time since she'd known him he seemed natural—

likable—and a little bit frightened, as she was herself, and trying to hide it.

He shifted. The crack in the planter widened a fraction.

"Look, I didn't get off to a very good start when I met you," he said, the words strained. "Would you promise me one thing?"

"What's that?"

His smile seemed a little crooked. Something in it touched her.

"If we both get through tonight in one piece, will you at least have a drink with me?"

"Will I be more useful in the wings or the audience, madam?" Rundell leaned forward, shielding his next words from Serafin's ears. "I brought my Mace."

Channing wasn't sure if he meant an aerosol can or a medieval club.

"For God's sake, leave it in here. Do you want to get us all arrested?"

They were in her dressing room. She flexed her hand, just released from the tape, and swabbed with alcohol to remove any traces of adhesive. It felt stiff.

"Just sit in the audience, Rundell. Enjoy yourself." She glanced at the clock on the wall. "Serafin and I have to get backstage."

Serafin seemed to feel her tension. He didn't chatter as usual as they walked down the hall together. She tested her hand again, then tried the film switch.

When they reached the wings, Serafin marched importantly and earnestly over to check the props on the side table she'd put in his care. If only they were granted the time together, he'd make a magician, she thought with a lump in her throat. Through a crack in the curtains she checked the house. Ballieu wasn't in the audience. Neither was the girl with long black hair who Ellery said looked to be Ballieu's helper.

It had been early afternoon when Ellery told her that, and they hadn't spoken since. She wondered how long it would take her after this show to get to Ellery's bungalow and be rigged with the wire. She went through her act automatically. Her mouth felt dry. What if Ballieu had made his move already? What if his promise to meet her had been a ruse?

"Hey, we're getting pretty good," said Serafin as they bowed their way off, and the next act was on.

"*You're* getting good with making that wand vanish," she answered. She managed a smile for him. "Look, I've got to check on something. Meet you back in the dressing room."

She walked as quickly as she dared, her black dress flapping against her ankles. At least it made her harder to spot by night, she thought. Except the damned sequins on it reflected any spark of light. Her hand rested on the hilt of her *kunjar* as she crossed the dining terrace and turned down the path to the bungalows. There were still people everywhere. But no Ballieu. No woman with long hair. The sounds from the lodge faded as she neared the bungalows. Alert for movement anywhere around her, she turned up the footpath to Ellery's and a moment later knocked on his door.

"Bill? Hey, Ellery, open up."

Efficient as he was, she was surprised he hadn't been watching for her. His porch light was on. She stood nervously outside the golden pool. There was no answer, no sound of movement inside.

It had seemed unthinkable to carry the .38 while she went onstage. Or maybe that had simply been rationalization. Maybe she'd wanted to deny she could bring herself to use it. Now she cursed silently.

The draperies at the windows of the bungalow were closed. A gentle testing with her fingers showed the door was locked. She wet her lips. More coolly than she'd thought she could, she lifted the *kunjar* from its sheath. With her left hand she drew a pin from her pompadour and picked the lock, then, with a burst of movement, kicked the door.

It crashed back, and there was no sound or movement from inside. The lights were on. The attaché case with the receiver in it sat open. Surely Ellery wouldn't have left it like that unless he'd had to move out quickly.

Then her searching eyes saw the old gold pocket watch. It lay between the bed and the nightstand, almost hidden. Ellery's good-luck piece. The one he always carried.

She ran and knelt to retrieve it. The crystal was shattered. A few feet away, on the carpet, she saw confirmation of what she was starting to fear.

It was a crumpled piece of cellophane. She brought it to her nose. The scent that lingered in the candy wrapper was faint but unmistakable.

Peppermint.

Twenty-three

She knew—more or less—what she'd find in the listening post. It was only a question of who. Her mind had worked of its own accord, and she'd snatched up keys in Ellery's room. She put the proper one in the lock and turned.

Walker's sizable shape was sprawled within sight of the door. Channing stepped over it, checking the bathroom, but he was alone. Kneeling, she felt for a pulse in his neck. There was none. He was facedown, shot in the back of the head. He would never see the grandchild he'd been so anxious about.

"You son of a bitch!" she said aloud, her whole being hardening as Max's stylish image swam in her memory.

Max, ever joking, ever trying to come on to her, was their traitor. This afternoon he'd nearly won her over with his moment of pensiveness—and it had been as calculating as the rest of him. Now he and Ballieu had Ellery.

Or had dumped him somewhere.

Channing pulled back sharply from the thought. Racing to the radio gear, she searched for a switch marked "send" and threw it. That was how you worked this type of equipment, wasn't it?

"Oliver? Can you hear me? Can anyone hear me? This is Channing. Walker's dead."

She pushed the switch back to the "receive" position. Nothing.

"God*damn!*" she said, her voice catching.

Twice more she tried, then gave it up. She ran the two flights up to her own room, too desperate to wait for an elevator. She'd left her key in the dressing room, but as that fact assaulted her, the door swung open.

"Channing!" said Serafin in surprise. He held up a book in his hand. "Okay if I borrow this?"

She pushed past him, peeling out of her costume and reaching for slacks as she spoke.

"Find Rundell. Stay with him. And tell someone I can't do the second show. Tell them I'm sick."

She was stuffing her shirttail in. Serafin's eyes followed her as she strapped on her *kunjar.*

"Channing?"

His voice was a child's voice, filled with fear and uncertainty. She swung from loading what she needed into her jacket and saw his heart in his face.

"You gotta come back, Channing!"

He was moving to do as she'd ordered, but his eyes clung to her.

"Promise," she said, and managed a smile.

As he left, Channing jerked a drawer open. Grim resolve overcame her last bit of reluctance. Glad of its cold impartiality, she took out the small .38.

"What the hell do you mean, my answer's coming in from Interpol?" barked Oliver Lemming, looking up from the map over which he'd been pouring.

"I haven't talked to Interpol. I never asked any question."

Irritated and increasingly tense that the evening was this far advanced with no word on Ballieu's movement, he rose from in front of the radio, tuned to the units at Palacio Sol. He moved stiffly but swiftly into the adjoining room where a telex had been installed. Three men he'd handpicked for this assignment were waiting and smoking. The one who'd summoned him, still in training, looked scared now. Everybody knew that when the old man moved as if he had a poker up him, he could be a bear.

It was hot in the room, and a little noisy from an ineffectual air conditioner. The men had dark stains under their armpits. One stepped aside, and Oliver read the message coming over: "Photo of female identified as Annette Lewis matches telephoto of Khadija Mansur, suspect in embassy bombing."

"Holy hell!" swore Oliver Lemming. "Start the chopper!"

The name had registered; he knew what this meant. His own outfit had come up with zero on those photos Ellery took, only Ellery hadn't been willing to settle for that. The boy was bright and had played a hunch. He'd gone to another source.

The fact that he had, and that he hadn't gone through Oliver, told Oliver plenty. It told him Ellery also believed what Oliver had begun to suspect: Whoever had stolen that piece of film might work for the State Department itself. It would explain why Ballieu had always seemed to be one step ahead of them. Ellery must have reached the same conclusion. Thorough professional that he was, Ellery hadn't been willing to discount even Oliver, himself, as the possible traitor.

Now Ellery could be in deep trouble, this crucial bit of information missing when he needed it. Ballieu must be moving tonight, but there'd been no word. That could be because someone had blocked the transmission. Or it could be because Ellery didn't know whom to trust.

"Contact the tail team. Contact Ellery!" he snapped, reaching for the holster he rarely wore anymore.

One of the men working under him leaned in from the other room.

"I just tried both, sir. Neither answers."

Oliver felt a wave of self-loathing hit him. He'd given Ellery this job because Ellery was as good as they came. Abraham packing Isaac off as a goddamn sacrifice.

He'd chosen Max and Walker because they'd followed the surveillance of Yussuf's network closer than most. And because they'd both been eager, he thought bitterly. Walker because he was starting to pine for promotion to a desk job, and Max to redeem himself for that slight blunder in Atlanta—or so he'd reasoned. Now it looked as though he'd sent Ellery right into a serpent's nest. Moreover, he'd endangered an innocent woman who'd agreed to be part of this because she possessed a basic sense of justice and responsibility that was starting to be in short supply these days.

"Keep a good grip on those hounds!" he ordered as rifles were snatched up and the four of them sprinted out into the night accompanied by a pair of bomb-sniffing dogs.

Knowing Ballieu was waiting on some sort of in-reverse time bomb, the dogs had seemed like a good precaution for when they reached wherever they were headed. Now, with no idea at all where that might be, Oliver wondered whether he and the three men with him had any chance in hell of helping William Ellery and Channing Stuart.

The moonlight jeered at her as Channing ripped up the narrow road in Ellery's car. The terrain looked unfamiliar coming at it in this direction instead of on horseback. From the moment she'd seen that watch in Ellery's room, her mind had seemed to be working on two levels. On one she'd forgotten she didn't have her jeep. On the other she'd snatched up those keys from Ellery's room, and she'd known where his car was parked, so she hadn't lost time.

If she and Ellery had been wrong about where the film was locked up, she had no chance at all. But she would play the chance she had. She wasn't going to let Ellery end up like Tony.

A tear slid down her face. For too long she'd pretended freedom from loneliness. She'd pretended neither time nor desire for the primal bonding between male and female. Now she knew she'd been deceiving herself as easily and completely as she deceived an audience.

Quelling the tightness in her throat, she fought the fear inside her until it was transmuted into anger. *She was not going to lose someone she cared for again!*

Automatically she tested her right hand. It felt normal. But then it had felt quite normal this morning when she'd dropped the coffee.

There was no one but her to go against Ballieu and all he stood for, and against Max's deceit. She was a Stuart, called to give a single performance that would prove her worthy of her heritage.

Ahead of her lights she saw a steep drive angling down. It would be the one to the clinic. She let her car glide past, let the engine die naturally, and got out.

Thanks to her work in hydrology, she had passed the night in desolate places more than once, and she was generally unafraid. This time, however, she knew the darkness was less than neutral. Either Ballieu or Max—or both—must have lookouts posted somewhere out here. The act of swallowing was hard, yet came involuntarily.

Up to this point sheer determination had blocked out every thought that might have restrained her. Now, analytically, she acknowledged she was into something over her head. It seemed to her a poor excuse for not moving forward. As cautiously as she could, and avoiding the drive, she began to climb.

The .38 in her right hand felt unwieldy yet comforting. Her eyes tried to pierce the shadows. She moved from the shelter of boulder to boulder, the slowness of her progress making her want to gnash her teeth. At last she glimpsed the line of a roof and, a few moments later, an entire side of the former Desert View Clinic. It was three-storied, solid-looking. There were bars on the windows. A faint light shone in an upper room.

Swallowing again, Channing began to pick her way toward the side of the building, avoiding the main door. She paused, her senses scanning the darkness for movement or sound. All she could hear was the drumming of her own blood. Was its loudness an illusion, like something seen-yet-not-seen performed onstage, or would real sound be audible? She held her breath, then started forward again.

Another endless flow of seconds, and then contours took form ahead of her, dismayingly identifiable. A swimming pool, with a high chain-link fence, abutted this end of the building. She gritted her teeth to keep from swearing aloud.

Entry, if she could make it, might have to be over echoing concrete here. The back of the building would surely be guarded. No choice remained but to backtrack as carefully as she'd come, setting course for the opposite side.

She did not see the shadow until it sprang. Brutal arms drove down to knock the gun from her hand. Channing reacted instinctively, slicing her elbow back and up into someone's belly, stepping sideways in a vain attempt to knock her attacker off-balance.

But she was in the hands of a trained fighter. She was spun around, kicked in the groin, whirled again by the scruff of her neck. She glimpsed a face—the sullen young woman with long black hair. Some species of long-nosed automatic rifle glinted in her hand. Channing almost froze.

Instead she seized the woman's wrist and tried to

slam it against the boulder at her back. A stronger arm resisted her own, and some part of the rifle smashed against the side of her head, momentarily dazing her.

Channing staggered, aware the woman was behind her, aware she was losing. She tried to fight, but her whole right arm was wrenched up behind her, pinned there by the woman's left hand. Then, in the course of a second, Channing felt the barrel of the rifle plunge deep into the opening of her ear.

Twenty-four

"I would love to kill you, American woman!"

The words hissed into Channing's left ear. The barrel of the rifle stabbed unrelentingly into the other. Its cold invasiveness created a terror of which Channing hadn't known she was capable. She couldn't force herself to open her eyes.

"Ballieu was so sure you were harmless—so sure you would do nothing without the man," the voice at her head continued. "I'm going to shove you into his teeth! I'm going to show him what a fool he is!"

She gave Channing a vicious shove, and Channing stumbled. The woman twisted her arm still higher. Channing cried out.

But the rifle was out of her ear now, merely pressed to her temple. Gasping, Channing allowed herself a single sideways glance at its menacing shape and the arm that was holding it.

Her free hand stole to her waist. It closed on the hilt of her *kunjar.* She had to regain her breath. She had to remember she was a Stuart, faster and more sure with her hands than most members of the human race. She had to remember Tony. And Ellery.

The training of her hands through her lifetime had made her almost ambidextrous. In a single lightning-quick move she brought the J-shaped knife free of its sheath and up. Its curved inner edge drove into the underside of her captor's forearm and jerked it upward. There was a sickening feel of blade against bone. A shriek from the woman behind her. The rifle sputtered bullets ineffectually as it fell to the ground.

Channing spun, behind her attacker now. She jerked the woman's good arm up as hers had been jerked, and pinned the blood-wet inner curve of the *kunjar* tight against the woman's throat.

"One move and your neck will feel worse than your arm," she said. In a flash she knew she was capable of what she was threatening. "Take me inside."

The woman in front of her was keening, cursing in Arabic, trying to clutch her injured arm against her body. It wasn't spurting. An artery hadn't been severed. Recalling the maimed child who had died in her arms in Beirut, Channing found she almost wished her aim had been better.

"You'll never get inside!" the woman spat.

"Move!" Channing shoved her.

They stumbled along like two members of a chain gang. When they reached the front door of the old clinic, the woman in front of her started to call out. Channing tightened the *kunjar* against her throat. The woman's words to whoever was inside were muted and terse.

The door opened. Two men, one with a mustache, one with a beard, leveled ugly little rifles like their colleague had aimed at Channing.

"Let her go," said the one with the mustache.

He spoke slowly and with a thick accent. Channing shoved the woman free.

"Sure. Just take me to Ballieu."

That was all she had wanted. She was in. She was still alive. She could do what she'd been sent to do. If they'd killed Ellery, her switch of the film would be for him.

The terrorist with the beard gestured toward the knife in her hand. She had no choice but to drop it. The men caught her on either side to drag her into a dim main hall.

"I need a tourniquet!" The woman gasped.

The sneer on the man with the beard made Channing fear she might never reach Ballieu.

"There's something about that film Ballieu doesn't know," she said, addressing herself to the one with the mustache. "If you don't take me to him, he'll have your heads when he finds out!"

They merely looked at her. Like carnivores, not people.

"I have friends out there!" she said curtly.

"She's lying!" said the woman who had attacked her. "There are no others."

She had pulled off a scarf and was trying to tie it around her arm.

The man with the beard caught Channing and began to push her up a flight of stairs.

Ellery had been drifting in and out of consciousness, but now he tried to maneuver his fingers up to the ropes he felt binding his wrists. He'd been dumped in a chair. He couldn't remember much that had happened since Max had jumped him there in the bungalow. He'd sensed something and turned an instant before Max's gun hit his skull, but the blow had dazed him.

Max had worked him over pretty well after that. Or maybe it had been Ballieu. They'd wanted a hostage, or they would have killed him. Ballieu had been pissed about something—that Max had jumped ahead of schedule and they were having to move out early. They must have been in this place several hours, waiting until they could open the safe.

Fuzzily Ellery realized he wasn't making any progress with the ropes. His muscles were rubbery. His movements were uncoordinated. And he heard voices in the room with him. He wasn't alone.

Abandoning his efforts, he tried to fix on his surroundings. He was in a large room, bare except for a desk and a couple of chairs. Ballieu stood behind the desk. Behind Ballieu, in the back wall, a huge vault large enough to step into stood half open.

Ellery forced his sluggish eyes to focus. What was Ballieu doing? Just finishing a look at the film, it appeared, examining it with a loupe. As Ellery watched, Ballieu put the small magnifying glass away and very carefully deposited the film he was holding in a padded envelope.

"A pleasure doing business with you, Ballieu."

That was Max's voice.

His field of clear vision enlarging, Ellery saw Max standing at one corner of the desk counting stacks of money into an attaché case. He flourished one bundle as if tipping a hat. It was evident from Ballieu's expression that Ballieu didn't like him.

Son of a bitch, Ballieu and I have something in

common, thought Ellery, his anger reviving him. Stinking Max. Wisecracking, good on the job—and a turncoat.

"Well, look who's joining the party," Max said, noticing him.

Max's eyes were bright. Ellery knew there was no good humor in his needling now, only malice. Maybe it had always been there, underneath.

"You know, Billy," Max said cheerfully, snapping the lid on the attaché case. "If you weren't such a straight arrow, I might have cut you in on this. We've always been good together. And it seems like such a shame, one man having all this money."

"Yeah. I can see you're torn up," Ellery said. There was pain in his lungs—as though he'd swallowed water somewhere along the line. He realized his clothes were soaked. "What did you do, Max, plan to jump those couriers or just stumble across them?"

He hated to give Max credit for planning that well.

Max sauntered toward him.

"Hey, I'm not the criminal type. Opportunity knocked and I answered. I'd spent all afternoon in that stinking meeting listening to people say how good *you* were after I'd had my ass chewed. When I started to my car, there came the couriers . . ."

With childlike playfulness he made a gun with his fingers and pantomimed firing—twice.

"Seemed like a wise career move."

Tense and straining for the first sound of the helicopter that was to come for them shortly, Henri Ballieu watched with increasing contempt the posturing of the American who had sold him the film. The man played. He was irresponsible. He had beaten his fellow agent beyond what was necessary, simply for his own satisfaction, then thrown him into the pool outside so he'd revive just to hear this crowing. The sort of personal indulgence that made a man prone to failure, Ballieu thought.

There had been an interval at the start of this night when Ballieu himself hadn't been completely confident of success, despite his planning. Mildred Farrow had called, weeping, to say she'd sprained her ankle and couldn't keep their date. Just at the moment when he might need one, he'd been short a hostage. Almost immediately the phone had rung again, and the American turncoat announced tersely that he'd just taken care of his partner and was leaving for the bungalow—ahead of schedule.

Ballieu had been furious at the American's rashness, but things had gone smoothly enough. Now strength was pounding in him. An old vitality had returned, for he knew he stood on the brink of success. A helicopter had been hired in a nearby town with orders to fly in at a precise time as part of a movie being filmed at this location. With a gun to his head the pilot would not object to flying them across the border. Very little could go wrong at this point, yet relaxing too soon, gloating over one's victory, would be the sort of mistake made by the crooked American.

The door opened unexpectedly. Ballieu whirled, catching up the automatic that lay on the desk beside him. His alertness quickened as he saw the Stuart woman shoved through the doorway by the two men who had arrived this afternoon to help him. Ballieu had left nothing to chance. He had thought it prudent to have men and weapons on hand in case he encountered American authorities once he had the film.

"She was outside," said one of the men. "She had a knife. She attacked Khadija."

Ballieu saw at their heels the sullen female who had opposed him at every step. Her arm dripped blood.

"You were so sure she was harmless!" She sneered, her face contorted by rage and pain. "You were too soft to deal with her, Ballieu!"

He saw the sneer give way to fear in the split second that he raised his pistol in her direction and fired. The arrogant little she-dog who had snapped at his heels fell with barely a whimper, shot through the throat.

The act gave him satisfaction. He had proved how soft he was. Even to her.

"She never would have survived the trip. She would have slowed us down," he said coldly, glancing down at her body.

The gun in his hand shifted toward the Stuart woman. His gripped tightened. "And you, you work for the State Department!"

The smile of the woman facing him was almost seductive in its challenge. "The State Department thinks so. Even him."

She nodded toward the traitor, ignoring the man they'd taken hostage as completely as she ignored the body that had fallen. This was some tactic of hers. It had to be, Ballieu thought. Yet her boldness was a thing of art, a thing that he could admire, even knowing he'd end it.

"You trust him, don't you, Ballieu?" Her words purred in her throat. She tilted her head back. "You'd better look at that film again."

Ballieu felt a silken thread of doubt curl through him. The other agent, the one named Ellery, looked stunned and uncertain. Max, flushed with rage, began to move swiftly toward her.

"What the hell—?"

"Max is part of their plan," she said, cutting in, her eyes flicking toward him.

The man tied in the chair tried to heave himself up.

"Shut up, damn you!" Ellery shouted.

Ballieu's gun swung toward Max Hopkins, halting him in his tracks. The man's joviality was deserting him, Ballieu noted. With his guards picking up his unspoken order to keep the man in his place, Ballieu once again trained his automatic on the *magicienne.*

"I thought you were an imposter, Ballieu," she was continuing, moving calmly and steadily closer to him, toward the front of the desk. "I just found out that isn't true. The State Department had been watching Yussuf for months. When they approached me and asked me to help them, I thought it was a trap."

"Fascinating," said Ballieu.

He was disappointed in her. He had thought her almost his equal. This fabrication of hers was as flimsy as paper. Yet her eyes had hardened.

"You'll think 'fascinating' if you don't listen!" she

snapped. "The film in that safe was a fake. There never was any film stolen."

The traitor started to lunge at her.

"You lying—"

A brief veering of Ballieu's gun both stopped and silenced him. The woman stopped, too, but she hadn't finished what she had to say.

"Give me the film, Ballieu. I'll show you the flaw. I'll show you how they set it up so immigration officials can spot members of your group."

"You'll burn for this!" threatened the man in the chair. One of Ballieu's guards was restraining him now.

"This is crap! They're playacting—both of them!" Max Hopkins said desperately.

"Keep him quiet," said Ballieu.

The guard with the beard brought his weapon up, aimed at the man who'd sold the film.

Ballieu listened for the *hélicoptère* and was startled to find himself thinking in French. It was happening more of late. He wondered why. He found the pain in his belly less troubling too. It burned constantly now, but he was achieving a victory over it. As he would triumph over this flimsy attempt to deceive him.

Raising the automatic, he pointed it directly at Channing Stuart's head. He motioned her forward.

"All right," he said affably. With his free hand he reached into his jacket to bring out the film in its envelope. "Show me."

The guard with the mustache, at a glance from Ballieu, had also trained his rifle on the woman who stood before them.

"May I get a magnifying glass?" she asked.

Ballieu almost smiled.

"Here," he said, freezing her as she started to reach toward a pocket. "I have a glass."

He extended the loupe he himself had used. She received it with her left hand, Ballieu noted. Her right hand reached for the film. Ballieu followed each small movement with his eyes.

"Watch her hands!" he said sharply to the guard with the mustache. "She likes to make things disappear."

He could hear her breathing. He looked at her face. Her eyes were dark and tried to draw his, but Ballieu, with an effort he found surprisingly hard, resisted. She was a consummate performer. He wanted to see the extent of her nerve.

Her hand, with the loupe between thumb and second finger, dodged slightly out. The rifle in the guard's hand jumped at the movement. Ballieu felt his own reflex copy the motion. A second faster on her part and she would have been dead.

Her hair shone around her like some aura of the powers she pretended to possess. Her eyes, as he glanced at them, held a strange and unsettling brilliance. Smoothly her hands began to move toward each other, the one with the loupe turning over, the one with the film giving an authoritative flick. She held the loupe over the film.

"There," she said, offering both to him. "See the final stroke of the last letter? It's too large."

Ballieu pretended to go along with her. He balanced both pistol and film in one hand and studied it closely. Accustomed to living with treachery for most of his life, he took the precaution of really inspecting the film, of moving his skilled engraver's eyes across the width of every stroke. Without comment he returned the film to its envelope and then to his pocket. He had seen no flaw.

Suddenly the side of his gun hand smashed out against the side of the woman's face and sent her sprawling. He felt the release of pent-up tension. Again she had tried to make a fool of him, as she had from the very beginning. He had wanted to bed her.

"Lies!" he spat. "All lies so you could get close enough to get one of our guns and free your boyfriend."

Ellery had made a last desperate attempt to free himself, but a rifle butt in his belly had stopped him. He had struck his head. Still tied to the chair, he lay unconscious on the floor.

Ballieu's straining ears picked up a sound.

"Helicopter's coming," Max said, still flushed with anger but swaggering forward to reclaim his place as an equal.

"We've no need of hostages now," said Ballieu, jerking his head toward the other Americans. "Shoot them."

"Hey, now. That's no way to treat Billy." There was malice in the traitor's face. "He'd rather go out with a bang. The lady deserves to squirm a little too. She's got too good an opinion of herself. Let's just set this little firecracker for them."

Removing the explosive charge once wired to the vault, he held it out.

Ballieu looked impatiently back from confirming

that the helicopter was the one he expected, not some sort of trouble arriving. The disposal of those left behind was of no consequence to him.

"It's your neck if they get away," he said.

The crooked American was crossing into Mexico with them. It had been a part of their deal. He planned to spin a story of being Ballieu's hostage, say he'd escaped, return to his position of trust. If he succeeded, Ballieu's organization might at some future date buy information from him.

"Getaway in ten minutes?" He snorted and knelt, resetting the timing mechanism and placing it at Ellery's head. "Old Billy's good with a bomb, but not that good. Especially with his hands tied. I want him to think of me while he's lying there feeling the seconds tick past."

Max Hopkins's teeth glinted fanglike in the uneven light. He patted the man on the floor.

"Guess we finally know which one of us was better, huh, Ellery? Remember me."

He rose and snatched a rope from the hands of one of Ballieu's men, who was starting to tie the woman. She was struggling furiously.

"That's too easy for her with the tricks she knows," he said. "There's a couple of straitjackets left in that closet where the scrub buckets are. Get one of those."

He grinned.

"Sorry, Channing. Guess I'm jealous. Thought you might take a shine to me."

He played, an overgrown child indulging his feelings, thought Ballieu irritably. Feelings were the thing to master, the beginning of competency.

For a brief time in the afternoon, he had almost forgotten that lesson. He had felt fear. He was starting to bleed from the rectum. Standing in the lavatory, no longer able to deny the fact that his life was leaking away, a fear of failure and weakness had welled up inside him. Then he had simply set it aside. He had reminded himself of his soldier's training, that he would think nothing of pushing on with blood seeping out from a wound in the leg or gut. Now he felt the film in his pocket, watched the jacket brought from the closet, and savored the taste of success.

By the time Channing Stuart was strapped up like a madwoman, the jacket around her torso and ropes around her feet, the helicopter was landing. Pistol in one hand, assault rifle in the other, Henri Ballieu led the way to the rear of the aircraft.

He waited until the door opened, then stuck the rifle barrel under the arm of the pilot who stepped out. A great breath of victory swelled him. He felt young and strong. He had accomplished a nearly impossible job. His name would be remembered.

"We are a liberation army," he said proudly. "We will not hesitate to kill you. You will do exactly as we say. You will fly us to Mexico."

Twenty-five

All the nerves in Channing's body seemed to end and sputter inside her head as she heard her captors' footsteps fading away. She was bound and helpless and probably going to die, yet a single thought danced defiantly in her mind: She had succeeded. Neither her hand nor her nerve had failed. She had proved herself a Stuart. She had reclaimed her birthright.

The pounding of her own head deafened her. Then she realized it was the time bomb ticking. She realized that exhaustion and panic had claimed her momentarily. Now she rallied against them.

"Ellery!"

He lay on his side, still unconscious.

"Ellery!" she said more frantically.

With her arms restrained as they were, she couldn't even pull herself across the floor. The straitjacket didn't leave her an elbow for getting a grip. And Ballieu's men had tied her ankles with the rope they didn't use on her hands.

She rolled. The body of the woman who had once been her attacker lay directly in her path. Repulsed, and reliving the coldness with which Ballieu had killed, she steeled herself and went over.

"Ellery!"

As she nudged him, his eyes slowly opened. Outside, she could hear the sound of the departing helicopter.

"You've got to get this unfastened!" she said, turning over to show the ties of the straitjacket. "Use your teeth. Use your tongue!"

Everything in her background told her the ties would yield more easily than the ropes binding him. If he could just free her, she could get them both out of here.

Twisting, she saw his eyes, still glazed, move toward the bomb. Nine minutes remained. He shook his head in an effort to clear it, then bit into her restraints.

A moment later he rolled back in defeat.

"It's no use, Channing. I don't know what the hell I'm doing. Why'd you come?"

"To switch the film—remember?"

As she spoke, she began to struggle rhythmically inside the jacket. In childhood she'd tried a few times to escape a jacket like this, but she'd never gotten adept; she had theory but no real practice. Desperation drove her.

Ellery pushed wearily up on his elbows. His eyes were dark with things unsaid. And with the inevitability of the outcome here.

"You almost made it," he said. "But we're not going to outrun this thing."

Vain as it was, Channing felt herself snap with indignation.

"What do you mean, '*almost* made it'? I *did* make it, Ellery—if you mean switching the film."

He blinked. He had started to work at his own bonds.

"When?"

She let a grin fly, even though her lips were bleeding from the way her teeth were grinding into them in concentration.

"You were watching. Didn't you see?"

She switched the method of her wriggling. The jacket seemed to be tightening, rather than loosening, around her. Ellery staggered to his feet.

"I'm going to break down that door. I can slide the bomb down the hall with my belly."

"No, dammit, Ellery! Don't try to be a hero! Even if you get through the door, there's an iron gate on the other side—maybe fifteen feet farther. It'll be locked too."

If he went, she knew he would never make it back. Tears were blurring her vision. For she knew that if she were going to die, she wanted it to be like this, half arguing with this particular man.

"Please." The words almost stuck in her throat. "Stay with me, Ellery."

For an instant he hesitated. His eyes held hers. With a lightning-quick, decisive motion he turned and kicked a chair to its side, then bottom side up. Straddling it, bearing down with his rope-bound hands, he tried to pry a leg loose from the metal strip that held it.

The dial on the time bomb said eight minutes were left.

"Channing? Serafin? Open up! It's Oliver Lemming."

Oliver pounded on the door some balding hotel lackey had pointed him to after no one answered in

Channing's room. Oliver and his team had descended on the resort like demons, flashing credentials while their helicopter waited with its motor running. Each discovery had added more weight to that already crushing his shoulders. Walker dead. No sign of Max or Ellery. Channing vanished before her final show of the evening. What the hell had happened here? Was he too late to save any of them?

The door opened and he saw the boy. Behind him stood a pinch-faced, elderly man he remembered from the house in Altadena.

"What's happened here, son?" Oliver bent and dropped a hand on the boy's shoulder to convey the urgency he felt. "One of our men upstairs is dead. There's no sign of the others. Where's Channing?"

For several seconds he thought the kid might hold out on him. There was something uncommon about his manner for one so young. And his eyes were strange. They'd been scanning Oliver's face as though it were some sort of book. Now they went distant. Dark. They gave an eerie impression of looking straight through Oliver, the walls, everything.

"That old clinic," the boy said suddenly. "We found it this morning."

"If Dr. Stuart's in trouble, you had flaming well better get her out," snapped the old man, hustling toward them.

Oliver nodded. He spoke again to Serafin.

"Can you show us the way?"

One of the men who'd accompanied Oliver came huffing up from the lobby. He spoke in gasps. "The dogs needed walking. We gave them a turn through some shrubs by the pool. They went crazy. Found enough plastic explosive out there to blow this place sky-high when the trigger wore through!"

Oliver's insides turned over. He set off for the stairs, not willing to chance the elevators. His concern was beyond the professional level. Had been all along, he realized. He cursed himself. He'd trade his own life for young Bill Ellery's. And Channing Stuart's.

Something in the way she'd looked at Bill that first day had made Oliver hope she might not only do the job, but also prove a good match for Bill in more ways than one. Bill deserved that.

Now, running, Oliver Lemming couldn't outrun the dread that the plan he'd conceived, which had seemed so reasonable at the outset, could be responsible for both their deaths.

"My father—could get out of one of these—in under two minutes."

Channing fought and bunched at the straitjacket. Strands of hair had plastered themselves to her forehead. She seemed to have changed position inside the folds of canvas, but time was going to defeat her, Ellery thought. Four minutes remained on the clock.

He pushed himself to continue his futile sawing at the ropes behind him by watching her face. No fear showed there, only fierce concentration. And a wounded professional pride, he recognized with a final amusement that choked as it passed over him. If he could just figure a way to get her out of this alive, then running second to Reid all his life would be okay. If he couldn't, his one prayer was that she'd still be this lost in concentration when the time ran out.

"Another minute—and I think I'll have it!" Channing said, panting.

But Ellery saw the clock hands on the timer slip to three.

When the bomb went off, it would take out this whole floor. Maybe more. He knew by the size of the charge wired to it. Savagely he bore down on the half-sawed rope that held him and heard it snap.

He rubbed his wrists as he flung the loops off and rolled over on his belly. His hands felt numb. His fingers grasped the bomb expertly, and he felt its rhythm.

In his mind he could see every wire and turn of its circuitry. He knew its intricacies. New as it was, he knew his fingers could probe and coax it apart. Except for one thing. This configuration of wires grew extremely sensitive to tampering as it approached the moment of detonation. They'd already crossed the margin of safety. If he tried to disarm it now, he could blow them both up.

He spoke aloud the words that were in his mind. "It's too late."

Channing had ceased her struggle, but now she resumed it. Ellery rolled to his feet.

There was one particle of a chance remaining. He couldn't untie Channing's feet in time, and he couldn't carry her far enough, but maybe he could get the bomb out.

Charging like a football player, he threw his

weight against the locked door. The old wood splintered. Another hit, the shock waves traveling through his chest to his healing wound, and the door gave way.

Two minutes. Racing back, he jerked over Khadija's body and grabbed the pistol he'd seen at her waist. With his hands tied, it had been useless. Maybe not now.

"Roll into the vault. Pull the door closed behind you," he ordered.

Carefully, as slowly as he dared, he picked up the bomb in his left hand, held firmly at his fingertips. Maximum shock absorption. Keep it as isolated as possible from his body's movements.

"Like hell I'll hide—" began Channing, still writhing inside her straitjacket.

"Roll!" he shouted.

Ignoring the sweat that wanted to pour from him, and moving as cautiously as possible, Ellery moved across the room and through the open door. If Channing survived, she could put out the word on Max. If she survived, she could tell Oliver the film had been switched.

The iron gate loomed in front of him. Channing was right. It had been locked. He stepped back and fired at the lock, braced mentally for a larger explosion.

There was only silence, and the ticking of the bomb in his hand. He dared not look at its timer now. Dared not even think. The corridor ahead of him seemed endless. There was a window at the end.

Ellery had the sensation of someone else walking

down the empty hall, not him at all. The someone else tried to move with speed but was hampered by the need for caution. His limbs were made leaden by the burden suspended ahead of him.

Ellery knew that the someone who planted his feet so carefully was moving toward his death. Yet he moved with determination. What would it be like, the end, when it came?

Channing's hair, and a picture of her hands as they moved, came to him. The freckles that sprinkled her forearms. The way she liked to roll her sleeves.

She'd been right. Nothing ever really vanished. Almost from the first, no matter how he'd struggled against it, the desire to risk facing what he felt for her had been there.

He had reached the window. There were iron bars over it. Calmly, detached now from the seconds trickling out to make way for a roaring, instantaneous death, he shoved the butt of the pistol he still held through the bars and smashed the glass.

Nervelessly he let his left arm slide into night air and dropped the bomb. He watched it hit the dark waters of the swimming pool below and sink.

Dazed, he brought his attention up to the window in front of him and moved back a step. He was alive. Breathing raggedly, he retreated another step, another step, still staring at the window with a sense of doom.

Then the explosion hit.

The force of it flung him down the corridor. He felt himself hit the floor. Part of the ceiling fell.

Debris bombarded his shoulders, his legs, as he brought his arms up to protect his head.

At last there was only dust settling. He heard sound first, the slapping of a helicopter coming in. Almost afraid to look, he raised his shoulders. He turned his head toward the room where they'd been imprisoned.

She stood in the doorway.

Free of the straitjacket.

"I told you I could get out in another minute," she said.

Twenty-six

". . . and the king of hearts is upside down."

Channing concluded her trick and sat back in her chair in the Magic Castle. It was a private club, a hangout for professional magicians where she'd spent many an evening with Gramps once she was old enough to be admitted. Some of the men who sat at the table with her, or stood making approving sounds around it in the gracious old upstairs bar, had known her forever and welcomed her back like a prodigal. To others she had been introduced as the Great Sebastian's granddaughter. Everyone seemed to know she'd just finished a two-week run of her own at Palacio Sol.

Two weeks, she thought. Incredible that she'd stayed and finished it like a real engagement. But she'd had nothing better to do, and performing after all these years had been like a tonic.

"That was Yussuf Bashim's trick," someone said as she gathered the cards.

Her smile was faint but steady.

"Yes. He left it to me."

They didn't know about Yussuf. They never would. And the part of him that had been good, the part of him that had been their valued colleague, would live on through her each time she performed this effect with the cards.

The tape that had caused her so much trouble, the trick that Yussuf had left her, had proved a part of him had been genuine. In the end, his friendship for her had been real. His love for magic had been real. She never could forgive what he'd been, let alone understand it. Still, the invisible things represented by that tape gave her a certain peace.

"Drink, Channing?" asked one of the men at the table.

She shook her head.

Restless now, she excused herself and stood up, hugging the sleeves of the dark green dress she'd found in a shop two days ago. It had pockets in all the convenient places where they were usually missing in women's apparel. It had seemed like an omen, a promise of new beginnings. Yet in spite of the dress, Yussuf's trick, and the warmth being offered her here tonight, she felt adrift. She wandered past the dining room with its stained-glass windows and ceiling fans, past the theater where a live show was in progress, through happy murmurs of conversation, and back to the bar again.

She had come here to meet Oliver Lemming. He was late. It annoyed her. But she knew her irritation was directed at herself and the wisps of emptiness that kept creeping up on her when she was unwary.

She hadn't seen Bill Ellery since the night he'd saved her life more than two weeks ago. Even before he had picked himself off the floor after the bomb blast, Oliver and other armed men had burst in. There had been a fury of questions, shouted orders, and suddenly, as Serafin pressed close to her and someone asked for the third time if she was all right, Ellery was being hustled away toward the helicopter. He'd looked back at her.

She'd thought he was about to pull away and cross the room to speak to her. He hadn't. She'd thought she'd hear from him the following morning. She hadn't.

Now she realized she'd probably never see him again. Logical, of course. Whatever had sprung to life between them had been colored by the danger they'd faced. Both of them were old enough to realize that. It was better this way. And less complicated.

Yet the knowledge was forcing her to face something she didn't want to see. It was more than her estrangement from magic that had driven her since she'd lost Gramps and Tony. She had gone from country to country, from challenge to challenge, filling her time, filling her head with thoughts so she wouldn't be forced to confront her own loneliness.

It was effective, she told herself. Maybe it was even healthy.

She could do it again.

She and Bill Ellery never would have worked out.

At one end of the bar a young man in full evening attire was doing the cups and balls beneath the approving eye of two older men. Two men at a table were challenging each another with their dexterity with coins. The little group she had left was exchanging card tricks. All the other women in the room were wives or girlfriends. Channing felt a keen and piercing sense of being a hybrid—an oddity of nature—alone.

Seeing Oliver's silver head appear amid the others in the room, she straightened herself and went to meet him. He had stirred her curiosity with his phone call yesterday. She had thought their business was finished, and all accounts settled.

"Say, this is quite a place," he said, looking around with almost youthful delight. "Would they have kept me out if I hadn't said the magic word to that owl downstairs?"

Channing smiled. Brief as their contact had been, she'd come to like this man. He'd been brisk yet concerned the night they had managed to thwart Max's plan for their premature funerals. Even as Oliver had stood in that deserted clinic barking orders, he'd scanned both her face and Serafin's for signs of strain. She had seen how his presence brought out the best in the men who were with him. She could understand why Ellery had been so torn by the possibility of his crookedness.

"How're Rundell and Serafin?" he asked as they settled down at a table for two with drinks in front of them.

"Fine. I broke down and bought Serafin his own setup for video games so I wouldn't go bankrupt. They're both getting pie-eyed playing them."

Channing sat forward, smoothing her sleeves again.

"Get to the point. Your department's paid for my jeep—and my other expenses. What's left to talk about? And why didn't you want to come to the house?"

She thought his eyes gave a twinkle.

"That little pitcher you took in has big ears. I thought things were better discussed somewhere neutral."

He leaned forward.

"I thought you'd like to know those phony passports have already helped nab some people intending to blow up part of an airport. They'll do a lot more good before Ballieu's outfit figures out what happened. Incidentally, there's a rumor Ballieu's in the hospital with some ailment and won't likely be coming out."

She was silent, trying to square her image of Ballieu with that of a man dying in an ordinary hospital.

"Any word on Max?" she asked.

"We've got him." Oliver's eyes betrayed a glint of satisfaction. "We're huddling with the Mexican government on an extradition agreement."

He looked down at his glass and frowned.

"This is a sales pitch, Dr. Stuart. You went in cold, and you did an amazing job for us. It's hard to find good people—men or women—for our kind of work. You've got what it takes. Bill thinks so, too, though I don't mind telling you he was skeptical when he first met you.

"What I'm leading up to is, would you go on working for us? It wouldn't be full-time. We'd want you to go on with your own work in hydro-geology. It gives you the kind of cover we couldn't invent if we had to. We'd want you to undergo some training first, and then we'd call on you whenever something came up where we could utilize your skills."

Channing formed her fingers into steeples and

thought about things she'd discussed with Ellery: a kind of global warfare. And she could make a difference. She'd be using her magician's know-how, not in the way her forebears had but in a way that suited her. She could feel the Stuarts of the past giving silent approval.

There was Serafin to consider, of course. She had responsibilities now. Yet she'd like to think it was partly for Serafin and other unknown kids that she'd agree to Oliver Lemming's offer. Maybe the reluctance to get involved was the very weakness on which people like Henri Ballieu counted.

"I'll do it," she said quietly.

Oliver Lemming sighed his relief and downed part of his drink.

"I ought to have some pretty speech," he said. "But the fact is, I don't know what to say except 'thank you.' It's from the heart, and from a lot of people who'll never even know they ought to say it for themselves."

Channing traced the rim of the table. She thought she kept her own question casual.

"Speaking of Bill Ellery, did his shoulder heal?"

She was thirty-two years old, but the man across from her looked at her as though he found her very young and very amusing.

"Why don't you ask him?"

He nodded toward the bar behind them. Channing turned and saw Ellery standing at the far end, eyes resting on her. All the poise she had accumulated over a lifetime slipped for a moment, and she was vulnerable. She felt the temperature of her body change from warm to cold and back again.

"Excuse me," said Oliver Lemming cheerfully, getting to his feet. "I forgot to feed my cat."

Ellery could almost read his boss's words, but too much of his attention was fixed on the woman now facing in his direction. She was as stubborn and enigmatic-looking as he remembered, Ellery thought. He watched her rise.

Oliver threaded his way out of the room, and then, even though there were people all around them, there were just the two of them. Ellery took a step forward.

She began to walk toward him. She was bristling. Holding herself very tightly. He understood that part of it. He'd vanished like one of the colored scarves she used onstage. He wanted her; he wanted to be a part of her life. Yet he knew he wasn't willing to give up his work, and a woman would have to be crazy to settle for what he could offer with that. Besides, he still wasn't sure how completely she'd gotten over her doctor.

He'd spent two weeks on recuperative leave, off by himself, fishing and thinking. Now he hoped the decisions he'd struggled to reach were valid.

They met in front of a vacant stretch of bar. Channing turned, planting her elbows on the solid edge behind her and leaning against it.

"I figured you were saying good-bye when you walked off without a word back there in that clinic, Ellery."

Her voice would have sounded steady to a stranger. But not to him. She didn't look at him.

"Yeah. Well. I meant it to be," he said.

Channing could feel him take a step closer. He was looking down at her hair.

"I got to thinking about what you said—about nothing in life being guaranteed." He turned and braced against the bar as she had done. His jaw worked once before he spoke again. "I need a partner for a job in Belgium next month. Wondered if you'd be interested."

His eyes were waiting as hers flashed up. They both understood it was more than professional involvement he was offering. He'd taken the first step, and it was scary for both of them. Instinctively Channing knew he'd never reached out to anyone before. And she'd lost Tony.

She grasped at safe ground, where they wouldn't have to reveal too much of themselves and where they could ignore the magnitude of the threshold they were crossing.

"I don't know. I've had a pretty good offer to look for water in the Sahara." She plunged a hand into her pocket. "Tell you what we can do. We can flip a coin."

Ellcry stared for an instant, then sparked with the realization that she was at least partly teasing.

"Uh-uh." His eyes were narrowing with mistrust. He detained her fingers in his, and she felt their intensity. "We'll use my quarter."

"Your quarter," said Channing agreeably.

An equilibrium was being struck—one they both understood, one they could modify through the years. They had been through a lot together. They would go through a lot more before they were finished.

A few of the bar's nearest occupants were turning to watch. Ellery rooted through his pocket.

"And I call," he said, pulling the coin he'd produced back as she was about to grasp it.

"You call," she agreed.

He paused.

"You can't be serious. You're going to keep up your work in geology? *And* do magic? *And* work for Oliver?"

"Well, I don't have a hobby, Ellery. Quit stalling." She took the coin.

She knew where she fit now. She was a Stuart. And she wasn't alone.

As Ellery watched, she flipped the coin. It glittered up in a shining arc, with Ellery's gaze nailed to it.

"Heads!" he said.

He stole a look at her. They shared a grin.

Ellery's eyes jumped back to the quarter.

It tumbled down and down.

And then . . . in front of Ellery's eyes . . .

in midair . . .

. . . it disappeared.